VESTA'S
SURVIVAL

STERLING R. WALKER

Vesta's Survival
©2021 Sterling R. Walker

Cover by Jessica Phillips
Models: Jared Weaver, Aaron Weaver

Disclaimer: All characters appearing in this work are
fictitious. Any resemblance to real persons, living or
dead is purely coincidental.

Printed in the United States of America

ISBN 13: 978-1-7366768-1-3

Science Fiction/Young Adult
First Edition
1 2 3 4 5 6 7 8 9 10

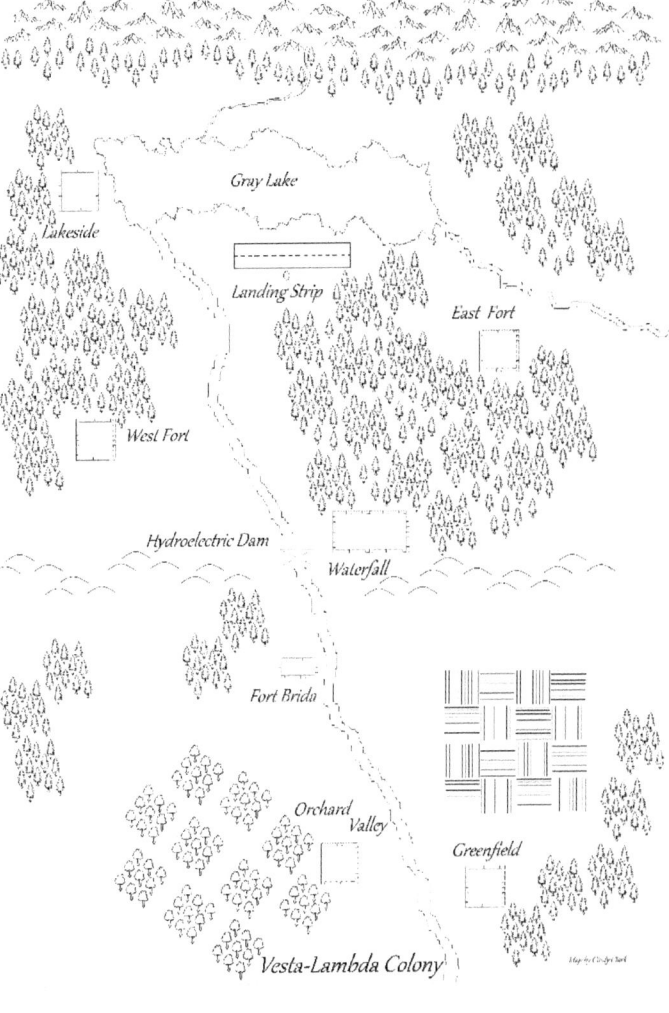

Gray Lake

Lakeside

Landing Strip

East Fort

West Fort

Hydroelectric Dam

Waterfall

Fort Brida

Orchard Valley

Greenfield

Vesta-Lambda Colony

Map by Carolyn York

ONE
NIGHT WATCH

"Darkness! Why didn't you tell me there were so many?" Corban Abrams drew in a sharp breath as he reached the top of the spiral staircase to the roof and caught a glimpse of the frightening scene three stories below.

"What are you doing here?" Thane asked.

"Couldn't sleep." Corban ventured onto the narrow catwalk, grateful for the handrails that allowed him to safely cross the rickety metal grating to Thane's side. Corban's older brother was standing in the middle of the span over West Fort's gateway arch. "Why aren't there any lights up here?"

"I keep meaning to ask Mayor Piroux the same question." Thane leaned his elbows on the railing and studied the chaos below with a detached expression.

The nighttime view from the catwalk was disturbing. Night terrors, dozens of them, gathered in the single spotlight in front of the gates, snarling and barking up at Corban and Thane, undaunted by the fact that their intended prey was ten meters out of reach. The vicious predators were large, with thick white fur like Earth polar bears, but hunted in packs like wolves. Night terrors were at the top of Vesta's food chain since nothing hunted them. The colonists killed them only in self-defense because the beasts tasted as bad as they smelled.

"I can't believe you have to stand here and watch them every other night." Corban shivered and zipped his jacket. The nighttime temperatures on Vesta rarely dipped below 21°C, but it wasn't the weather sending a chill down his spine. "Didn't you request a day shift?"

"Yes, but I have to wait until the head sentry changes the schedule." Thane sighed. "I think he's expecting volunteers, but nobody wants the night shift." He paused, staring down at the bloodthirsty predators. "It was a mistake for the Hunters Guild to ignore them. Their numbers have soared, and now they'll do anything for a meal."

"Even scale walls?" Corban watched in fearful fascination as one of the beasts stood on hind legs and scratched the gates with razor-sharp claws, its fanged muzzle dripping with saliva.

"If they figure out how to climb walls, we're all in big trouble." Thane fingered the hilt of the machete at his waist.

Corban wished he'd brought a weapon, but he'd gotten out of the habit of carrying one since he was no longer an apprentice in the Hunters Guild. "Did you mention to the mayor that this job gives you nightmares?" He thought back to the night eight storms ago when Thane saved him from a night terror. He glanced at the titanium brace his brother wore on his left leg over his cargo jeans. The brace replaced the kneecap Thane lost to the creature's deadly jaws that night.

"It bothered me when I first started working as a sentry, but I mute my hearing and don't really notice the stench anymore." Thane's Talent allowed him to hear things from great distances, but it also gave him the ability to tune in or tune out sounds at will.

Corban hadn't noticed the pack's rotten meat odor due to the overpowering scent of smoke. Not the woodsy, familiar smell of fire pits, but the acrid, chemical stench from the smoldering remains of the starship *Unity*, four kilometers to the north at the colony's landing strip. Without thinking, he took a deep breath, which triggered a bout of coughing. The smoke he'd inhaled yesterday, after the ship exploded, made breathing painful. Dr. Lorna DeKalb had assured him the congestion would clear in a few days, as would the stinging from the burns he and Thane received when hot cinders rained down on them from the collapsing ship.

Thane rattled off a few coughs of his own before changing the subject. "With you, not sleeping is a bad sign. Did you have a new premonition?"

"Not recently, no." Corban didn't want to disclose the details of his latest dream. His clairvoyance was a major source of stress since important details were always missing from his premonitions. He thought back to the dream where he first saw Nikki Ramirez, days before he met her in person.

Nikki. The thought of her eased his anxiety. Corban's rare second Talent, his empathy, allowed him to sense other people's emotions, but around Nikki, it was stronger and more precise. Their Talents had merged, sharpening their individual abilities and creating a unique mental communication between them.

"Limited source telepathy," was the unofficial diagnosis, but Corban preferred Brida Vaughn's definition. "Shared light." The young woman had seen something unique in their auras. Corban still didn't understand what an aura was, but he was grateful for Brida's Talent. Her advice to "choose what you want to see" was the catalyst Nikki needed to work past her fear of physical contact and learn to control her Talent for seeing other people's memories.

Eager to steer the subject away from premonitions, Corban asked, "How's Jing?"

"Really upset. Zhao arranged to have Kun interred in the Shrine today." Jing and Zhao Kaczenski's father was killed in the *Unity*'s explosion. Although the siblings had been estranged from their father for months, they were unprepared for his death. Thane and Corban lost both parents in the Plague sixteen storms ago. Corban was an infant at the time, too young to remember them, but he knew Thane would be able to empathize with Jing's grief.

Kun had attempted to abduct Jing to take her aboard the *Unity* with him. His plan was to use the ship to return to Earth. If he'd succeeded, Jing would've died with him, a thought that made Corban queasy. Her loss would've devastated both Thane and Nikki because Jing was Nikki's best friend.

"What about you?" Corban asked. "How're you feeling?"

Thane hesitated. "I feel like I need to stop being a coward and make a commitment to Jing."

Corban was glad he was gripping the railing with both hands so he didn't keel over. "What?"

"You heard me." Thane was uncharacteristically gruff.

"Did she use the *L* word?" Corban sensed his brother's nervousness. Thane didn't like to share his deepest feelings, so Corban knew this confession came with reluctance.

Thane blew out a long breath. "Yes, and I haven't been able to stop thinking about it since she said it. I can't stop thinking about her. I dread every moment we're not together. Is this what love feels like?"

"I don't know. I've been scraping my jaw off the floor ever since Nikki said it to me."

"She did?" Thane turned to face him. "And how did you respond?"

Corban studied his brother's features by the dim light of Vesta's stars. Thane's wavy blond mop and three-day-old scruff gave him a lazy appearance while his muscular shoulders, chest, and arms announced the opposite: Thane Abrams was a hard worker despite his damaged leg. He'd been a metal-smith apprentice before the internment.

"I didn't say anything," Corban said. "She took me by surprise."

"I almost drove off the road when Jing told me." Thane started to laugh, but it triggered another round of coughing.

Corban waited until Thane could breathe again before asking, "What kind of commitment?"

"The forever kind."

Whoa! "But Jing's only seventeen."

"You think seventeen is too young to fall in love? Sound familiar?"

Corban frowned. "I said that to you."

"And you were right." Thane turned to gaze down at the night terrors with a thoughtful frown. "Do you mind if I give her Mom's ring?"

"You're serious?" Corban was wide-eyed. "When are you planning to ask her?"

"Soon," Thane said. "She needs time to grieve of course. And I should probably mention it to Zhao, since he'll be my brother-in-law. But soon, maybe on her birthday."

Corban tried to wrap his brain around this confession. "Sure, you can give her Mom's ring. Nikki doesn't like jewelry."

Thane shot him a suspicious look. "So you're thinking about marriage too?"

Corban thought back to his last premonition. He'd been in Lakeside fort's infirmary, where he'd spent several days recovering from a fever, but this time he wasn't the patient. He was standing at the foot of his bed in front of the narrow window, but someone else was lying in it, sound asleep. None of the other beds were occupied. It was late, and the room was dark, illuminated by weak starlight through the single windowpane. He thought about turning on a lamp, but something made him hesitate. He had a feeling he shouldn't wake the patient.

He sensed peace and contentment, but it took him a few moments to realize those feelings weren't emanating from the patient. There was something warm cradled in his arms. He looked down and gasped. He was holding a newborn baby bundled in a soft blanket. All Corban saw in the poor lighting was a tiny face looking up at his with great interest.

Corban tore his gaze from the infant's bright eyes and moved to the side of the bed to take a closer look at the patient.

It was Nikki. She was lying on her right side, her long black hair splayed across the pillow and a look of sheer exhaustion etched on her face.

Corban looked down at the newborn again, his mind unable to process the shock. *I'm holding my own child!*

"I'm not ready." He wrenched his attention back to the catwalk and his brother. "But I know it will happen someday."

"Is this because you can hear each other's thoughts?"

Corban shook his head. "It's not just that. There's more, but it's hard to explain."

"Try me." Thane sounded impatient, but his next words conveyed genuine interest. "You look so happy when you're together, you're practically glowing."

"We do glow, on the inside. There's a light that fills us whenever we touch," Corban said. "We both feel it and see it in our minds. It's warm and peaceful, and we both miss it when we're apart. It's like we're two halves of the same soul. Sorry, I know it sounds stupid, but I don't know how else to explain it. We share a light, like Brida said."

"That sounds like love to me." Thane smirked. "A weird, supernatural kind of love. The rest of us ordinary mortals have to trust our feelings."

Corban snorted. "Well then, you'd better propose to Jing before her feelings change."

One of the night terrors issued an extra loud howl, interrupting the brothers' cheerful banter.

"They look hungry, don't they?" Thane sighed. "If you see Rupert, tell him to hurry up and relieve me."

"Will do." Corban made his way back to the spiral staircase. "Good night."

TWO
SOLONA'S ANNOUNCEMENT

Thane was standing in the noisy and crowded courtyard of Fort Brida with Jing by his side. She held his left hand, although she took care not to touch the blister at the base of his thumb or lean against his arm, which was peppered with burns. Jing miraculously came through the *Unity*'s explosion unscathed, even after being dragged one hundred meters across the ragged tarmac on Solona's lab coat. Thane was grateful Jing had been unconscious through the entire terrifying ordeal.

"How are you feeling today, *mei mei*?" Zhao Kaczenski asked. He was standing a meter behind them in the crowd.

Jing didn't turn around. "I feel like I'm going to punch you if you don't stop asking. I'm fine, *ge'-ge.'* I'm sad about *Baba*, but I'm fine."

Thane smothered a chuckle, determined not to annoy Zhao. He nodded over his shoulder at the younger man.

Zhao slouched, with arms folded, studying Jing's back with a concerned frown. He was taller than his sister, but not by much. Zhao's black crew cut stuck up at

8

the crown of his head, and the pale circles beneath his eyes stood out against his bronze complexion. He worked with Thane as a West Fort sentry, along with Isaac Nomura and Rupert Conquist, Thane's best friend. The four young men shared Leighton Abrams's old apartment, along with Corban, who was learning the herbalist trade with Nikki and Jing's supervision. Thane was envious of how much time Corban got to spend with Nikki at Lakeside's apothecary six days a week.

He gave Zhao a sympathetic nod before turning to face the makeshift platform in the center of the courtyard. Nikki's mother, Solona Zegarelli, was seated in a wheelchair on the tiny stage, her right thigh bandaged from hip to knee, and pain clouded her features. He had no idea why she left the hospital ship so soon after being shot, but he suspected she was almost as stubborn as her daughter.

The petite nurse's auburn hair sported singed patches, and small bandages covered the assortment of burns on her arms. Solona's son-in-law, Fort Brida mayor Derek Graham, stood next to her wheelchair. His dark skin and coarse black crew cut contrasted with Solona's pale complexion.

Frieda Moul, a Stray with a Talent for projecting her voice, was also on the platform, preparing to speak for them so everyone inside the fort could hear.

Scanning the crowd for familiar faces, Thane also tuned his hearing to locate familiar voices. Three levels of apartments, which formed the fort's exterior walls, had windows facing the courtyard. Hundreds of people leaned out of these windows, eager to hear from Solona, who was a respected leader in the colony as a tireless advocate for the Strays.

Thane slipped an arm around Jing's shoulders and

drew her closer. She tilted her head back to look at his face. He didn't mind that she was short; the top of her head reached his sternum. He did mind that her small, dark eyes were red and puffy, but nothing he said would comfort her. She needed time to grieve.

If Kun Kaczenski had succeeded in getting Jing aboard the *Unity*, she would've died too, a thought that made Thane feel as if a heavy weight filled his chest. Solona had intercepted Kun outside the ship and wrestled an unconscious Jing away from him, and this was after Nikki's father, Elian Ramirez, shot Solona in the leg. Thane was grateful for Solona's courage.

He suspected this gathering would be more than a formal expression of sympathy for the Stray-haters who'd been determined to return to Earth in the ship despite Corban's premonition that the *Unity* would explode on liftoff.

"She's probably going to remind us about the vaccine," Jing whispered. Thane had no trouble hearing her by tuning out the din of conversations around them.

"Darkness." He'd forgotten about the Zegarellium issue. The native plant Solona discovered by accident had been a miracle cure for the deadly Plague that cost Vesta half its adult population sixteen storms ago. Now it was a curse for the daughters of those who'd survived.

"Good evening, and thank you all for coming at such short notice!" Frieda's amplified voice silenced the crowd. "Mayor Graham has a few words to say about the tragedy two days ago, and Solona Zegarelli has some counsel for us."

Derek spoke in Frieda's ear. Thane almost tuned in with his Talent, but decided to hold off and hear the news at the same time as everyone else.

"Those who chose to ignore Corban Abrams's premonition paid with their lives. Thanks to Nikki Ramirez, we have a list of the eighteen who were aboard the *Unity* and one who was too close to the ship when it exploded."

Derek handed Frieda a datapad, and she read off each name. The crowd was silent for a few moments after she announced the final name. "Herbalists Guild Master, Kun Kaczenski. His was the only body recovered from the site."

Jing sniffled once but otherwise didn't react. Thane wondered if she'd finally cried herself dry. He heard Zhao sigh behind them. Thane understood how painful it was to be an orphan. Even as an adult, he missed his parents with an ache that never went away.

Derek continued. "Let's pray some good will come from this tragedy, that the loss of these nineteen colony leaders will convince the other Survivors to accept us. Three forts have invited us back and even requested we use our Talents to benefit the colony, but the other three forts remain anti-Stray, although that may change when Waterfall and East Fort elect new mayors. Solona and I will continue to advocate for those of you who want to return to your homes and guilds. Those of you who wish to remain in Brida are, of course, welcome to stay and build new lives here. We'll need three or four more months to complete construction on the remainder of the living quarters."

Mayor Graham nodded for Solona to take over. Frieda leaned down so she could hear Nikki's mother before addressing the fort.

"I'm sure you've heard rumors about the side effects of the Zegarellium vaccine, but I think it's time I explained the facts." Solona's brow furrowed, but she continued speaking without pause.

Frieda repeated, "Normal girls born to Survivor mothers do not have uteruses. As far as we know, Normal males are fertile, but it makes no difference if Normal females can't conceive. Females born to mothers who *didn't* have the vaccine will be able to add to the population. To be blunt, the future of the colony is in jeopardy because only Strays can have children."

The population of Vesta colony was divided into three distinct groups: Survivors, adults who lived through the Plague, thanks to the Zegarellium vaccine; Normals, children who weren't exposed to the Plague or were born after it was eradicated; and Strays, children who were below the age of puberty during the Plague and exposed to it. The virus caused the Strays' DNA to mutate, making them immune, but as a side effect, giving each a unique mental ability called a Talent.

Thane thought about how his abusive uncle Leighton Abrams had organized the forced exile of the Strays from the rest of the colony to Seventh Fort, a primitive structure built in secrecy under Uncle's direction. Following the internment it was renamed Fort Brida after the young woman Leighton murdered during the roundup. Now the exiled Strays were the best hope for the colony's survival. The irony wasn't lost on Thane.

Uneasy muttering arose from the crowd. Jing squeezed Thane's hand again. He assumed it was to remind him she'd received the vaccine. It didn't make a difference to him because he loved her, although he hadn't worked up the courage to tell her yet.

"Although two children has been the average for many couples, in order for the colony to survive, it's crucial that each couple has *five or more* children and that you start as soon as possible, especially you young women of childbearing age."

Jing wasn't the only one to gasp, "Five!"

"There are no more ships coming. Earth made that clear after the Plague by severing all contact with us. The *Unity* found us by accident. It was supposed to land on another colony. The grim reality of our situation is that in order to have enough workers to provide the food and services we need to survive, Strays must increase the population."

Solona's next words to Frieda were short and terse, causing the younger woman to blush. "Get busy and make babies! If you choose not to reproduce, our population will decline to unsustainable numbers and die out."

Shocked conversations erupted as the Strays absorbed Solona's words.

Watch and listen. You might learn something. Rupert Conquist's voice interrupted Thane's thoughts. His best friend could send mental messages to anyone from any distance.

Thane looked around for red hair and spotted Rupert not far from where he and Jing were standing. Rupert was elbowing his way through the crowd, trying to get to someone. People moved aside for him until he reached his goal: Yasmin Wang, a Medics Guild apprentice and member of Brida's community council. Rupert had been seeing Yasmin for two storms.

Thane's jaw dropped as he watched his friend get down on one knee in front of Yasmin, and focused his Talent in time to hear, "Would you do me the honor of becoming my wife?"

Yasmin's mouth was open too. "Yes, as long as you promise to *never* quote poetry to me again!"

"I promise," Rupert said.

The crowd surrounding them laughed and clapped

as the two embraced, sealing the deal with an enthusiastic kiss.

"That's how it's done!" Frieda added, "I'm available if anyone else feels like proposing!"

The courtyard rang with cheering and applause.

Jing stood on tiptoe but couldn't see over the heads in the crowd. "What happened?"

"Rupert proposed to Yasmin Wang."

Thane heard Jing whisper, "Lucky girl," under her breath.

"It'll be dark in an hour," Frieda said, "so everyone should head back to your forts! Thank you for coming!"

The wedding's in three weeks. Rupert's nonchalant message took Thane by surprise. *I guess Yasmin's been planning it for a while and was just waiting for me to ask. I'll need a best man.*

Thane caught Rupert's eye through the crowd and gave him a thumbs-up.

THREE
THE RECEPTION

Nikki turned around in the tiny bathroom, trying to see over Jing's face in the mirror. "What do you think? Is this too revealing?"

Jing paused, hairpin between her teeth, and studied Nikki's reflection. "You really think Corban will mind if you're showing a little cleavage?"

"It's a lot of cleavage." With both hands, Nikki gripped the scooped neckline of the tight-fitting blue denim dress and tugged it upward a few centimeters.

"Now you're showing too much leg." Jing smirked.

Nikki sighed, wishing she'd borrowed something else to wear. She hadn't worn a dress since her sister Eliana's wedding three storms ago. "Dagmar's shorter than me. This would fit you better."

"Every woman in the colony's shorter than you." Jing smoothed the waistline of her pink silk cheongsam, a traditional dress from her Chinese Earth ancestry. "No way am I wearing that. This was my mother's, and I've been waiting for a special occasion to show it off."

Nikki smothered a spark of envy. "It's beautiful, but

you know those slits on the thighs almost reach your backside."

"Good." Jing flashed a wicked grin and returned to pinning up her shoulder-length black bob, securing a pink peony blossom behind her left ear.

"Thane won't be able to take his eyes off you." Nikki found her comb and worked at the knots in her long black mane. "I don't know what to do with mine. I guess I'll put it in a ponytail."

"No, you won't." Jing snatched the comb from her. "Sit."

Nikki parked herself on the toilet lid and submitted to Jing's ministrations. Fifteen minutes of combing, braiding, and an excessive number of hairpins produced an impressive up do that seemed too fancy for the plain denim dress. "Thanks."

"You just need a necklace," Jing said.

"I don't own any jewelry." Nikki walked to the bedroom they shared in the Lakeside apartment that used to be Solona's and searched the wardrobe for her shoes. "What am I supposed to wear on my feet? All I have are work boots and walking shoes."

"And now you have sandals." Jing waltzed in behind her and reached underneath her bed to extract two pairs of bluedeer-skin sandals. "I ordered these from the Tanners Guild last week. Surprise!"

Nikki accepted the pair Jing handed her. "Thank you, they're beautiful!" She turned them over, studying the simple flat soles and twin blue straps. "How did you know my shoe size?"

"I traced the soles of your boots onto a scrap of paper. Try them on."

Nikki set them on the floor and slipped her toes beneath the straps. "They fit! Too bad my toenails haven't seen daylight in six months."

Jing laughed. "I think Corban will be too busy staring at your cleavage to notice your feet."

***

The dirt courtyard of Fort Brida was softly lit with torches and a few make-shift stone fire-pits for the Wang-Conquist reception, which would continue into the night. Guests like Nikki and Jing, who lived in other forts, had been offered overnight accommodations, a luxury Brida didn't have a few months ago when the structure was as primitive as a barn.

Nikki looked over the two picnic tables outside the main door to the dining hall. They were covered with platters of finger foods, a simple white cake decorated with fresh flowers, and a giant punch bowl, which was actually a wine barrel sawed in half. "Dagmar's baking is almost as good as her mother's." Cooks Guild master and West Fort's mayor, Gina Piroux, made delicious pastries.

Jing nodded. "Are those empanadas?"

"Samosas, maybe," Nikki said. "Whatever they are, they smell incredible."

"I wish we could fill a plate now. I'm starving." Jing's stomach gave a loud gurgle.

"I think we have to wait for the bride and groom to make an appearance before we can eat." Nikki rubbed her own hollow middle and led Jing around the Strays congregating near the make-shift dance floor, which was a partitioned off section of dirt swept free of debris. A six-member Artists Guild band was warming up on an assortment of hand-made drums, dulcimers, and wooden flutes.

"Where's Thane and Corban?" Jing asked.

"Just keep talking, and Thane will find you," Nikki said. "Or maybe he'll smell you. How much perfume are you wearing?"

"It's peony extract." Jing sniffed her wrist. "I made it myself. Too strong?"

"Smells like you went swimming in it. There's Corban!" Nikki broke into a big smile as he emerged from the dining hall, balancing a large tray of ceramic cups in his arms. He set his burden next to the punch bowl and walked over to join them.

"I was just helping Dagmar," he said.

Corban was more spruced up than she'd ever seen him in a purple button-down shirt tucked into brand-new gray pants. His blond hair was parted on the left, and he was clean-shaven, both rarities for him. Warm brown eyes, framed by unusual blond lashes, crinkled at the corners when he smiled, revealing a chipped front tooth.

"You look stunning." He wiggled his eyebrows at her.

Nikki reached out to embrace him, and he wrapped both arms around her waist. Warmth and light flooded her mind. She bypassed his memories, a feat she was unable to accomplish with anyone else, and reached the higher level of consciousness, which gave her direct access to his thoughts.

You're wearing a dress! he thought.

Eyes up here! Nikki nuzzled his smooth neck. *There's so many people, and they keep bumping into me. I'm already tired of seeing random memories.*

"Would you two please not do that mind-reading thing?" Jing stood on tiptoe, looking toward the door Corban had just exited. "Where's Thane?"

"Right behind you," a familiar bass voice said.

Jing whirled around, threw herself into Thane's arms,

and kissed him as if they hadn't seen each other for months, although Nikki knew they'd met for a picnic on the banks of the Cold River yesterday during Jing's lunch break. Thane's patchy facial hair was gone, and he'd gotten a crew cut. The ever-present brace on his left leg matched his gray button-down shirt.

Thane set her on her feet and gave her a slack-jawed once-over. "You look gorgeous."

Jing blushed as pink as her dress and beamed up at him.

"How was the wedding?" Nikki asked Thane.

"Short and simple. Just their families, roommates, and Pastor Martin from Lakeside to officiate. It took about ten minutes."

"Where's the happy couple?" Jing asked. "I want to see Yasmin's dress."

"I'm sure they'll be here before the gates close." Corban grinned. "We decorated a Medics Guild truck for the occasion."

"It turned out to be more trouble than it was worth. I sliced my thumb tying a rope around one of the cans." Thane held up his left hand, bandaged thumb still oozing blood.

"You poor thing!" Jing seized his wrist and examined the damage. "That looks painful. Do you need stitches?"

Thane looked embarrassed but didn't shy away from the attention. "It's fine. We'll be able to hear their truck coming from half a kilometer away. The cans were Corban's idea."

"Don't blame me. I told you not to string any cans with jagged edges."

"They *all* had jagged edges."

Nikki interrupted their debate by bursting into laughter. "You tied cans to the bumper of their truck?

Some traditions never die, no matter how embarrassing they are. I'm happy for Rupert and Yasmin. This will be the first of many Stray weddings, according to Mom."

Thane shot Corban a mysterious grin before focusing his gaze on Jing. "I'm not due to give the toast for a least an hour. Let's see what's in the punch bowl and find a quiet place to talk." He slipped an arm around her waist and guided her toward the picnic tables.

Nikki suspected those two wouldn't do much talking, but Corban distracted her. *Want to dance?*

The band struck up a slow tune, and several Strays moved onto the dance floor. *You know how to dance?*

No, but how difficult can it be? Corban led her to a spot near a pair of couples swaying to the music.

Nikki draped her arms around his shoulders and nestled her face against his neck with a happy sigh. *I've never danced with anyone before.* She'd avoided touching anyone up until the moment she'd saved Corban from his deranged uncle with one powerful swing of her sword.

Don't remind me. Think happy thoughts.

Like you—and me?

We haven't had much to celebrate until now, Corban thought. *Let's appreciate every minute we're together.*

Mind if I cut in? The new voice in Nikki's mind belonged to her brother-in-law, Derek Graham. His Talent, like Rupert's, was sending mental messages.

Did you hear him too? she asked Corban.

Yes, just like an echo. He's standing behind you.

Nikki reluctantly let go of Corban and turned to face Derek. "Do you really want to dance with me, or do you just need to talk?"

Derek arched a thick black eyebrow at her.

Nikki wasn't intimidated by his stern expression.

"Where's my adorable nephew?"

The mayor's face relaxed into a toothy smile. "Solona's babysitting Travis tonight so Eliana and I could attend the reception."

"I'm guessing you have something to tell Nikki that's not for my ears," Corban said.

Derek shrugged. "I'm sure it'd take you less than a minute to find Thane and ask him to eavesdrop, so you might as well stay. This is about you anyway."

"Me?" Corban frowned.

This time Nikki raised an eyebrow at Derek. "What's wrong? Is Corban in trouble?"

"Nothing's wrong. Why didn't you tell me Corban needed a place to live in Lakeside? He can have our apartment. It's been empty for months."

Nikki winced. "I didn't mention it because I assumed you and Eliana would move back." She didn't look him in the eye as she added, "Or at least Elie and Travis would."

Derek scowled. "You thought she'd leave me?"

"Brida wasn't fit for human habitation when we first came here," Nikki amended that to, "when we were *forced* here. I know I wouldn't want to live here even with all the improvements. It's not my home."

"You were only here for a few days. Elie feels differently about Brida now. It's our home, and we plan to stay. Our Talents are needed here."

"I'm happy for you." Nikki tried to sound sincere, but her opinion of the fort hadn't softened since the internment. She still thought of the place as a prison. "Are you sure your apartment wasn't assigned to someone else? I know the Kaczenskis's place was given to a family with four children last week. There's a long waiting list for housing, and I doubt Mayor Brooks would let a

21

single person have it." She shot Corban a sympathetic look.

"Why don't you ask Brooks yourself?" Derek handed Corban a pair of keys. "I'm sure she'd let you have the place if Thane lives there too."

Corban smiled. "Thane in Lakeside? He'll think his birthday came early. Thank you, Mr. Mayor."

Derek rolled his eyes, grinned, and walked away.

Corban put an arm around Nikki's shoulders. *Bertram Conquist, Rupert's uncle, was elected Smiths Guild master. Rupert and Thane hate being sentries and want to return to the guild. I'm sure Bertram would let Thane work at the forge in Lakeside.*

I know Jing'll be thrilled to hear Thane's moving into the same fort. We should go find them.

His mouth twisted into a sly grin. *It'll have to wait. Thane needed to talk to her alone this evening.*

Nikki laughed aloud. *Oh, he needed to talk to her?*

Corban's eyebrows shot up. *It's not like that! My brother would never take advantage of her.*

Well, Jing would be happy to take advantage of him. Are you sure we shouldn't go rescue Thane?

Corban was hiding something. She probed his recent memories, searching for a conversation with Thane.

Give up. Corban leaned in for a kiss, but she knew it was an attempt to distract her. *You'll find out soon enough.*

Find out what?

Corban laughed and pressed his mouth to hers. Nikki gave up and kissed him back.

FOUR
PARTY CRASHER

Thane's palms were sweaty, and he wasn't sure how to hide them. The cups of punch provided some condensation, so he hoped Jing would assume his damp hands were a result of the icy drinks. He took a big gulp of his delicious apple-grape juice, disappointed it wasn't spiked. He wanted something to steady his nerves.

Jing sipped her drink and allowed him to escort her up the staircase to the deserted second floor of the east wall. She didn't say a word, which was a rare feat for her, but her dark eyes were full of mischief. His eyes kept drifting to her legs. It was difficult not to stare when the sides of her dress were cut so high.

"I wanted to show you Corban's old room." It was a lame excuse, but he hoped she'd overlook his awkwardness.

They looked in the doorway to the former post-op room. Solona, Nikki, and Jing had camped out in the room to take care of Corban after Elian Ramirez shot him. The women had slept in blankets on the rough plank floor.

"Quite a difference," Jing said. "It actually looks livable now."

Corban's hospital bed had been moved to the fort's new infirmary, replaced by a double bed covered with a colorful quilt. There were curtains at the window, an overhead light, a wooden chair, and a braided rag rug on the floor. It was basic but more comfortable than before.

"The completed rooms have adjoining bathrooms now." Thane pointed to the newly framed door next to the headboard. "They've been working hard to finish the fort. You remember my room?" He steered her across the hall into the room he'd shared with Rupert and Zhao while Corban was recovering.

Jing looked around. "Not as nice as the courtyard rooms, but a huge improvement."

This room was furnished like the first, with a bed, rug, overhead light, and door to a bathroom, but the big difference was the addition of a window. A square had been chiseled out of the center of the stone wall. It was framed but there was no glass in it yet.

"The Glaziers Guild has been working overtime on windows." Thane closed the door behind them and set their empty cups on the nightstand. "They have fifty to go."

"I hope they finish before the storm. They'll need shutters too."

"The Carpenters Guild is working on those."

Jing walked to the opening and looked out at the exterior of the fort. She gasped and stepped back as a pack of night terrors spotted her and erupted in a frenzy of howls and barking.

Thane hurried to her side and wrapped her in a comforting embrace. She was trembling, so he drew her back to the other side of the room.

"Awful beasts," she muttered into his chest. "I hate that you're stuck watching them on sentry duty." She peered up into his face. "Do they still give you nightmares?"

He shook his head. "I try to ignore them." Which was difficult, considering the racket the bloodthirsty predators made from dusk until dawn.

Thane held her until the night terrors quieted a fraction. The setting wasn't ideal, but he didn't want to be distracted from the reason he'd brought her here. *Here goes,* he thought, fresh beads of sweat popping out on his forehead. He released her and took a step back. "Jing, there's something I want to ask you."

Jing's eyebrows shot up, and she glanced over at the bed, her mouth forming an *O* of surprise.

"No, that's not—" He was embarrassed she'd jumped to the wrong conclusion. "I didn't mean to—" he stammered.

Jing's *O* morphed into a perplexed scowl. "Then why did you bring me here?"

This wasn't going as he planned, and Thane struggled to gather his courage a second time. "So I could do this." He got down on his right knee and held her hands between his sweaty palms. "And ask you to marry me."

She gasped. "I thought you said you'd wait until I'm older"—tears filled her eyes—"to ask *Baba* for my hand."

"You'll be eighteen in a few weeks. I thought—" He studied her frightened expression, and the well-rehearsed words lodged in his throat. *She's not ready for a big step like this.* He let go of her hands long enough to reach into his shirt pocket for his mother's wedding ring.

Jing took one look at the tiny circle of golden metal set with three clear stones and started to bawl. Thane couldn't tell if she was shedding tears of joy or grief. Was he about to get his heart broken? He waited for her answer, trying not to appear desperate.

After a long pause, she choked out, "Isn't there something else you need to say to me first?"

His fear was replaced with confusion. "I should've said please?"

She glowered at him, then burst into laughter. "You idiot! You have no idea what I'm talking about, do you?"

"Sorry." He shook his head, stung that she'd call him an idiot even if he deserved it. "I need to stand. My leg's hurting."

Jing helped him to his feet, wrapped her arms around his waist, and flashed him a hopeful pout. "Three little words you've never said to me?"

Thane's face grew warm. "Oh, those words." He took a deep breath. "I love you, Jing Kaczenski. Would you please marry me?"

"That's better." She whispered yes and stood on tiptoe to kiss him.

"Try it on?" Thane asked when he was able to come up for air.

Jing held up her left hand and helped him slip the ring onto her third finger. It was a good fit.

"It was my mother's; it's been handed down for generations," Thane said. "My great-grandmother, Nia Abrams, wore it in her stasis pod on the first manned scout ship from Earth. I don't know what it's made of. The gold metal and gemstones aren't found on Vesta."

"It's beautiful. I'm honored to continue the tradition." Jing stretched to kiss him again but froze when the night terrors' howls abruptly increased in volume.

She turned toward the window. "They aren't normally this loud, are they?"

Everything Thane thought he knew about night terrors seemed inadequate as he focused his Talent on the cacophony of frenzied barking. Although he'd spent months on sentry duty listening to the monsters outside West Fort, there was something odd in the higher-pitched growls of this pack.

As he pondered the possible reasons, his eyes were drawn to the ring on Jing's finger before shifting to his own bandaged left hand. Understanding chilled him faster than a plunge into Gray Lake. "They smell blood!"

"What?" Jing gasped.

Thane reached behind his back, searching for the doorknob. "The blood from the cut on my thumb."

"Maybe we should—"

She didn't get a chance to finish the suggestion as a large white muzzle appeared at the window opening. The beast seized the ledge with its forepaws and snarled, flecking the room with foul-smelling saliva.

Jing screamed.

Thane was grateful he had a grip on the doorknob. The night terror scrambled to get its hind legs across the window sill, but Thane moved faster. He yanked Jing into the hallway and slammed the door behind them. "Run!"

"I'm not leaving you!" Jing tore across the hall into Corban's old room and returned in seconds with the chair.

Thane used his body to barricade the door, but the entire frame shook as the night terror threw itself against the other side. Jing propped the chair beneath the doorknob, but Thane knew it wouldn't hold the beast for long. "Find Frieda! She can warn the fort!"

Jing seized his hand and tried to drag him away from the door. "You're coming with me! If one was able to scale the wall, more will find their way inside!"

Thane hesitated, even as the night terror rammed the door again. The wooden frame creaked in protest. It wouldn't take the creature long to break through. He remembered something. "Brida's sentries have guns!"

"Then let's find one!"

Thane nodded, and they sprinted for the stairwell. He shifted to a long skipping stride, which put less weight on his bad leg, enabling him to move faster, and they were able to descend to the courtyard before the night terror broke out of the room.

"Night terror!" Jing screamed, but she wasn't loud enough to be heard over the music and laughter of the party in full swing. "There's a night terror inside the fort!"

Thane looked around frantically for something to barricade the door to the stairs, but Jing gripped his wrist. "Leave it! We've got to find Frieda!" He allowed her to take the lead while he shut his eyes and scanned the crowd for familiar voices.

"I hear her; she's over by the food!"

Jing changed direction, elbowing people aside to reach the buffet. "Take cover! There's a night terror inside the fort!"

"What?" Someone gave her an incredulous look.

"Where?" another Stray demanded.

Several people took up Jing's warning, shouting, "Night terror!"

"Where is it?" A sentry Thane recognized from an earlier visit to Fort Brida emerged from the crowd. She was wearing a holster over her dress, and her pistol was already drawn.

"Over there!" Jing screamed again as the creature

burst through the door to the courtyard.

"Night terror in the fort! Run!" Frieda Moul's voice drowned out all other noises, and a shocked silence descended over the courtyard as one hundred faces turned to discover the deadly party crasher.

Strays screamed and scattered as the beast charged, heading straight for the nearest people on the dance floor, Corban and Nikki.

"Nikki!" Jing shrieked as Thane looked on in horror.

A shot rang out, and the night terror slowed, a patch of dark blood appearing on its neck, but it didn't stop.

"Shoot it again!" Corban bellowed, placing himself between Nikki and the night terror as they attempted to flee, but there were too many people in the way.

The night terror snarled and lunged straight at Corban with gaping jaws.

It stopped mid-pounce, frozen on the spot like a huge, bloodthirsty puppet on invisible strings.

"Darkness!" Corban stumbled backward into Nikki. They clung to each other, shaking. The rest of the reception guests stared in stunned silence.

Thane exhaled, terror and relief flooding him simultaneously. "What just happened?"

Jing nudged him. "Look! It's Linnea."

Thane found it difficult to tear his eyes away from the night terror statue, which continued to snarl and snap at its intended prey but was unable to move its body. He forced himself to turn his head to see where Jing was pointing.

Linnea Savoy was standing near the dance floor, her eyes shut tight and a look of intense concentration on her face.

"She can't hold it much longer!" Jing's shout broke through the stunned murmurs of the crowd.

The sentry fired again, this time shooting the beast in the forehead. The night terror shuddered and went limp. It remained frozen in place a moment longer before collapsing to the dirt.

Thane gripped Jing's hand and attempted to steer her toward Corban, but she resisted, pulling him toward the buffet. "Others might be able to climb the walls. We have to tell Frieda."

He nodded, grateful she kept her head in a crisis. They parted the crowd to reach Frieda and found the newlyweds beside her, standing over the uncut wedding cake. Rupert was holding the cake knife out like a weapon, the other arm around his trembling bride.

"It climbed in through a second-story window," Thane explained to all three in a rush. "There may be more."

"Darkness!" Rupert exchanged a grimace with Yasmin. "Our new suite's on the second floor. Let me find Derek." He shut his eyes to summon Mayor Graham, who emerged from the crowd moments later with his wife, Eliana, Nikki's older sister.

Nikki and Corban were right behind the Grahams, white-faced and clinging to each other for support. When Linnea joined the informal circle, Jing rushed forward to hug her. "Thank you!"

Thane told Linnea, "You probably saved Corban's life."

"Thank you," Corban echoed in a shaky voice. "That's the second time I've been too close to one of those monsters and someone rescued me." He exchanged a significant look with Thane.

"But it wasn't just me." Linnea was tall and petite with straight, white-blond hair and a kind face. She was a member of Brida's community council, and Thane had witnessed her Talent before. Linnea threw her arms wide, indicating everyone in the crowded court-yard. "I don't have the mental strength to stop some-thing big. I think another Stray concentrated on it the same moment I did, but I don't know who."

"You acted in unison and stopped it?" Derek ap-peared dazed. "I can check the census to see who else is telekinetic. The spreadsheet's on my datapad."

"Darkness!" Nikki spoke up. "If Strays can use their Talents together, this changes everything!"

"What do you mean?" Linnea asked.

"I mean Corban and I aren't the only ones who can merge Talents!"

Thane wasn't certain what she was implying, but he ventured a guess. "Our Talents aren't limited to our personal use? We can use them with other Strays, like Linnea just did?"

"Yes!" Nikki beamed at Corban, who attempted to return the smile but still looked stunned from his close encounter with the night terror.

"Why hasn't anyone tried this before?" Jing squinted at Nikki. Thane imagined that, as a Normal, his fiancée was feeling left out of this amazing discovery. He hoped someone could help her understand.

Corban and Nikki gazed at each other, communi-cating silently for a moment before Corban replied, "With us, it was an accident. We had no idea it could be done, so we never thought to try it."

"Plus I had to practice for hours before I was able to hear his thoughts," Nikki added. "Our telepathic link is different from our regular Talents."

"Her access to memories and my empathy worked together somehow," Corban said. "But two Strays with the same Talent working together makes more sense."

"I acted on impulse," Linnea said, "and apparently

someone else did too."

"I wish they'd come talk to us," Derek said. "I'd like to see if it can be duplicated."

Frieda's laughter startled Thane; he'd forgotten she was part of the huddle. "For a brilliant community leader, you can be an idiot sometimes." She smirked at Derek before standing on tiptoe and announcing to the fort in her amplified voice, "Would the telekinetic Stray who helped stop the night terror please report to Mayor Graham at the buffet?"

Derek rolled his eyes. "I'm sure I would've thought of it eventually."

"Keep telling yourself that." Eliana slipped an arm around Derek's waist.

A tall and thin young man Thane didn't recognize walked up to the group. His skin was very dark, like Mayor Brooks's, and he wore wire-framed glasses over large brown eyes. "Did you want to see me, sir?"

"Yes." Derek drew him into the circle, shaking his hand with enthusiasm. "Who are you? Which guild?"

"Sergey Gupta, Teachers Guild." He sounded nervous, his eyes shifting from face to face, but his gaze lingered on Linnea's.

"Gupta?" Jing asked. "Are you related to—?"

"Yes, the Lakeside teacher everyone dreaded having for history," Sergey answered before she finished. "He's my father. Or he *was* my father before disowning me because I refused to leave the guild."

"I know how that feels," Linnea said. "My mother couldn't wait for me to turn eighteen so she could make me change guilds."

Sergey flashed a shy smile. "I was teaching at Orchard Valley Community School before the internment."

"We can get to know you later," Derek said. "Right

now please tell us if you've ever done something like this before."

"Could you do it again?" Nikki added.

Sergey shook his head. "I can use my Talent to move small objects. I didn't know I could move something large with the help of another Stray."

"We're grateful you did," Thane said. "You saved my brother's life."

"I'm just glad I was able to help." Sergey shoved his hands into his pockets and studied the toes of his boots. "Even if it was an accident."

Nikki bounced on her heels. "Do you all realize how many problems this could solve for the colony?"

"Let's not get ahead of ourselves," Derek said. "I agree this is incredible, but I need time to think. I should meet with the council to discuss the possibilities—"

"Time is something we don't have," Thane interrupted. "We've got to board up the second-story window openings tonight, or more night terrors might scale the walls. If one smelled the blood from my small cut, the whole pack will smell the blood from that." He nodded toward the disgusting carcass in the middle of the abandoned dance floor.

Derek bit his lip. "I'm not sure what we can use. Doors from the unfinished rooms, I guess, but it will take time."

"This can't wait for construction crews," Corban said. "We have the manpower right here in the courtyard."

Derek nodded and turned to Rupert and Yasmin. "Sorry to spoil your evening." He pulled Frieda aside and discussed with her what to announce.

Frieda moved a platter of cream puffs and climbed onto the picnic table. Her amplified voice could be heard above the clamor of nervous conversations. "We need every able-bodied colonist to form teams and find tools—hammers, nails, and screwdrivers. We need to board up all the exterior windows on the second floor, using the doors from the unfinished third-floor rooms. The sentries and anyone else with a firearm should spread out and protect the workers. Let's do this quickly before any more night terrors crash the party."

Without a word of complaint, the Strays got to work, dispersing in small groups to the four fortress walls.

FIVE
YASMIN'S TALENT

Corban, Thane, and Rupert decided to repair the door the night terror broke down. Nikki thought she'd be in the way, but she went upstairs with Jing and Yasmin to offer moral support.

"Are you sure you don't need our help?" Jing asked Thane in a tone Nikki took to mean *I don't want to get my dress dirty but feel guilty letting you do all the work.*

"It's fine. We can handle it." Thane winked at Jing before stooping to pick up the door. "Looks like the hinges tore free," he told Corban and Rupert. "Shouldn't be hard to reattach."

Jing sighed in obvious relief and turned to Yasmin. "Your dress is beautiful. What size is it?"

Nikki laughed. "She's half a meter taller than you."

"Dresses can be altered," Jing said. "I know someone in the Tailors Guild."

"You'll have to ask Mayor Piroux. It belongs to her, and she's hoping her daughter, Dagmar, will wear it someday. Let's go sit down." Yasmin lifted the sides of the skirt to raise the hem of her floor-length white gown—the neckline cut low to show off her brown shoulders and cleavage—and led them into Corban's old room. She sat on the bed, smoothed the full skirt, and raised a slender black eyebrow at Jing. "Who cares about dresses? Do you realize what merging Talents could mean for the Strays?"

"I do." Nikki leaned one hip against the footboard. "Corban and I have been practicing for months."

Jing pouted as she flopped down next to Yasmin. "I don't want to talk about Talents right now. Doesn't anyone want to hear what happened right before the night terror tried to kill us?" She waved her left hand in Nikki's face. "Aren't you curious what Thane wanted to ask me?"

"What's that?" Nikki seized Jing's fingertips to get a better look and instantly regretted it as her friend's memories invaded her mind. She let go before witnessing another argument between Jing and her late father. "Thane gave you a ring? Why?"

"It's an engagement ring!" Jing's cheeks turned pink. "Thane asked me to marry him!"

"Congratulations!" Yasmin said.

"That's great. I'm happy for you," Nikki managed after a pause.

Jing gave her a curious look.

"I wasn't expecting him to—" Nikki began.

"Neither did I!" Jing laughed. "He used to say I was smothering him, but I guess he likes it!"

"Rupert said married couples on Earth traditionally wear rings to symbolize their love. He plans to forge one from steel for me," Yasmin said. "His uncle Bertram wants to put him in charge of the smithy here."

"That's excellent," Nikki said. "Have you started working at the infirmary?"

Yasmin nodded. "I'm assisting your mom. She wants to train me in midwifery."

Jing pursed her lips. "Sounds like fun."

"You remember I helped at Travis's birth?" Yasmin asked Nikki. "Your sister had an easy time despite delivering during a storm. I tend to panic if there's any complications and need all the training I can get. Solona's hoping for a lot of babies from the Strays within the next few storms." Yasmin paused, her expression thoughtful as she looped a finger through a spiral of her long black hair. "I'm not sure how I feel about having five children."

"Me either." Jing squirmed in her seat as Nikki gave her a searching look. "I mean, I'm too young."

"You're childbearing age." Yasmin snorted with laughter. "Get with the program, Ms. Abrams."

"But I'm not a Stray!" Jing said. "I had the vaccine and can't risk having any girls because they'll be infertile."

"I'm afraid science hasn't found a way to guarantee gender." Nikki tried to sound sympathetic but failed. She didn't want to think about motherhood, not when she'd barely reached adulthood. The thought of being responsible for a completely helpless human being filled her with anxiety.

"I'd be fine with five sons, I think." Jing rubbed her bare arms. "They come one at a time, right?"

"Usually," Yasmin said. "Although Rupert's father was a twin, so odds are that he and I will have a set." She shuddered. "Let's talk about something else!"

"Good idea. Let's talk about Strays being able to merge their Talents." Nikki turned to Yasmin. "Speaking of Talents, I don't know what yours is."

Yasmin pursed her lips. "It's so strange I don't use it often. I have an enhanced sense of taste."

"So you can identify which seasonings the cooks use in the food?" Jing asked.

"Not that kind of taste." Yasmin hesitated. "I can

taste things in the air."

Nikki squinted at her. "How does it work?"

"Watch." Yasmin shut her eyes and stuck out her tongue.

Jing and Nikki exchanged a puzzled frown as Yasmin turned her head from side to side, as if trying to catch raindrops on her tongue. Nikki was reminded of an article she'd read about an Earth creature called a snake. Snakes used their tongues to explore their environment and locate prey.

"I taste blood in this room." Yasmin opened her eyes. "And urine, vomit, morphine, and vegetable soup."

"This is Corban's post-op room." Nikki nodded. "All those things were in here."

"But that was months ago." Jing winced. "You *taste* urine and vomit?"

"I'm not using my taste buds, so it's hard to explain," Yasmin said. "There was also lavender here, and ginger, and thyme."

"You know your herbs. Those were essential oils we used to treat Corban." Nikki grinned at the nurse with newfound admiration. "You can sense what was here a long time ago?"

Yasmin bobbed her head. "I can taste what's here now, like wood, stone, and fabric, but anything that used to be here leaves traces too. I've used my Talent to locate things on the hospital ship."

Nikki nodded. "I remember Mom mentioning she needed rubbing alcohol, and it took you two minutes to find a forgotten bottle in the back corner of a linen cabinet four levels up."

"Some tastes are so strong they're easy to locate." Yasmin shrugged. "It takes concentration, so I use my Talent only when I need it. It comes in handy for medical diagnoses."

Jing said, "You can tell if someone's been poisoned?"

"Yes." Yasmin smirked at her. "Right now I taste peonies."

Nikki nodded. "You don't need a Talent to tell Jing doused herself in it."

Jing scowled as Nikki and Yasmin laughed.

***

Thane poked his head into the room fifteen minutes later. "We're all done, ladies. The fort is secure."

Jing sprang to her feet so fast that Nikki laughed. *It's going to be a short engagement.* She watched her friend rush into Thane's arms as if she hadn't seen him for weeks.

"We sealed up the window opening, using the bathroom door." Corban appeared in the doorway next to Thane. "It's the only wood we could find."

Yasmin got to her feet. Nikki walked beside her, at a more dignified pace, into the hallway.

"The room isn't safe if a night terror managed to scale the wall outside," Thane said. "We turned the bathroom door sideways and nailed it to the window frame. That should hopefully keep any more out."

"You don't want to see the mess the night terror left." Rupert was brushing off the lapels of his gray suit jacket as he joined the huddle. "The room will be off limits for a while."

"Where are we supposed to stay tonight if so many rooms are boarded up?" Nikki looked down the hall where a dozen Strays were leaving the exterior rooms with hammers and other scavenged tools.

Rupert smirked. "I don't know where you four are staying, but Yasmin and I have the honeymoon suite."

Yasmin's brown cheeks took on a rosy hue. "It was nice talking to you," she said to Nikki and Jing.

"Thanks for showing us your Talent." Nikki slipped her hand into Corban's and tried not to grin like an idiot as warmth and light filled her mind. Now that they realized some Talents could be used together, she wondered if other Strays would discover a mental connection like the one she shared with Corban.

He squeezed her hand in response. *I'd like to think it's just us.*

"I'm sure Derek and Eliana are already working out accommodations for the guests," Jing said.

"Probably women in one room, men in another," Thane said.

Nikki tried not to laugh at Jing's pout.

"Congratulations, again, on your wedding." Thane pulled Rupert into a one-armed hug.

"Thanks for being my best man," Rupert said. "I'll understand if you already have a best man for your big day." He gave Corban a thumbs-up.

Thane gaped at his friend. "You know? I thought I was the one with the hearing Talent."

Rupert shrugged and slipped an arm around Yasmin's waist. "Your bride-to-be has a lot of volume."

"You can say that again," Corban muttered.

"My future brother-in-law better have *nice things* to say about me!" Jing wrapped both arms around Thane's waist and shot Corban a scowl.

"Yes, ma'am," Thane and Corban said in unison and burst into laughter.

***

"Here you go." Eliana opened the door to an interior room on the first floor of the west wall.

Jing peeked inside. "Two twin beds?"

Eliana shot her a suspicious frown. "It's for you and Nikki. There's towels and soap in the wardrobe. Thane, Corban, come with me."

Goodnight, Corban gave Nikki a quick kiss before releasing her hand. Jing and Thane's goodnight kiss took so long that Eliana cleared her throat several times.

"See you tomorrow," Thane said, as Corban dragged him down the hall after Eliana.

SIX
MOVING DAY

"We've got to cull the night terrors," Solona announced to the assembled group in the Waterfall community council room. She sat at one end of the long oval table and surveyed the seven seated mayors, representing each of the forts. Most of the colony's guild masters were also present in chairs lining the walls. The room was crowded.

"Their numbers have grown so large that we're all in danger," Derek said.

Corban stood in a corner behind the chair of Smiths Guild master, Bertram Conquist. Although Corban was the only colonist at the meeting who didn't hold a title, it wasn't difficult to convince Nikki's mother to let him attend as a former member of the Hunters Guild. He scanned faces, gauging the mood of the room to determine whether the attendees were taking Solona's announcement seriously.

"There's no reason to go looking for trouble." Lakeside mayor Pavitra Brooks, normally one of Solona's staunchest allies, responded first.

"They only come out at night," Greenfield's mayor,

42

Afshan Qualls, added. "That hasn't changed in the eighty-seven-storm history of the colony. We're safe inside the forts."

"We're not safe anymore. The beasts are starving because they can't find enough food," Solona said.

"It's true," Sentries Guild master Athena Yarborough spoke up. "Night terrors have wiped out the local bluedeer herds, and now they're hunting any type of prey. They've been terrorizing the goats and sheep in the stone barn, trying to break in."

"They can climb walls now," Solona said.

"Impossible," Brooks said.

"One of them climbed in a second-story window of Brida last night," Derek said.

Brooks gasped. "How? What happened?"

"Leighton Abrams had the fort built so fast, the walls are rough and easy to scale," Derek said. "A creature hungry enough will find a way in, and one did."

The mention of his abusive uncle stirred up painful memories. Corban suppressed them with effort.

"We boarded up the second-story windows since currently they're just holes in the walls," Derek said. "Not that a pane of glass will keep out a night terror."

"The Stray communication teams in each fort have been reporting to me for months." Yarborough spoke over the skeptical murmurs. "They think the night terrors are trying to find weaknesses in the walls. Even if you sleep so soundly you haven't noticed the increased howling at night, you must've noticed the claw marks on the gates and first-floor window sills. There's evidence they've been at the landing strip, trying to claw their way inside the Shrine."

"I thought the first ship was airtight," Brooks said.

"Not airtight enough." Yarborough pursed her lips.

"Don't forget the recent funerals. The Shrine's been opened several times the past few months."

Brida Vaughn, Corban thought, *Uncle, Kun Kaczenski. Even the twenty original passengers in the* Unity's *stasis pods were interred in the Shrine. There was nothing left to bury from the eighteen colonists inside the ship when it exploded.* He pushed the grim thought aside.

"Night terrors have never been seen at the landing strip before." Orchard Valley's mayor, Faith Ann Jesperson, sounded worried.

"Thane Abrams heard them the night the *Unity* exploded," Derek said. "Even the smoke wasn't keeping them away. They're getting bolder. We were fortunate the one that got inside Fort Brida was stopped before it hurt anyone."

Too close for comfort. Corban heard Derek's voice in his mind. He was impressed the mayor sent thoughts and spoke aloud at the same time.

Derek turned to West Fort mayor Gina Piroux. "All your sentries need to be armed like the ones at Brida. A staff or machete isn't enough."

"Rupert mentioned it to me just before his wedding." Mayor Piroux narrowed her eyes at Corban. "At the rate my communications team's being reassigned, West will need new sentries as soon as possible."

"We're working on it." Solona inclined her head toward Guild Master Yarborough.

"The sentries should shoot the ones outside the gates." Corban's suggestion drew shocked looks from the group.

"They're attracted to blood," Solona said. "That kind of carnage would bring more of them to the forts."

"Maybe," Corban said, "and yes, it would be a big mess to clean up in the morning, but I think it would be the safest way to cull the ones threatening the forts."

"I don't think we should eliminate a few at a time. We need to target their lairs and kill them all," Derek said.

The muttering grew louder. Corban sensed the growing apprehension in the room.

"We don't know where they live." Brooks scratched at the red dot painted on her forehead. "We don't have enough firepower to kill entire packs. It would be too dangerous to confront them in their lairs."

"Waiting until they find their way inside the forts is more dangerous," Solona said. "We've ignored the threat for too long."

"What do you propose?" Brooks asked.

"We should arm the Hunters Guild," Derek said. "Send them out in groups to locate the lairs in the daytime and kill them while they sleep."

"How can hunters find them?" Brooks sent Derek a suspicious frown.

Derek hesitated. "There are Strays who could locate them by scent."

"No!" Medics Guild master, Lorna DeKalb, spoke for the first time. "I already lost my husband on the *Unity*. You're not risking my son's life too."

"It was Fenton's idea to volunteer his Talent." Derek wouldn't meet her eyes. "Everyone would be well armed."

Dr. DeKalb shook her head, her lips pinched into a thin line. "It's too dangerous."

"It needs to be done." Solona's firm, no-nonsense tone quieted the room. All eyes were on her. "Night terrors are clever pack animals. One figured out how to climb a wall, and more will follow. Don't you live in a second-floor exterior apartment, Lorna? Are you willing to wait and see if a night terror gets hungry enough to pay a visit?"

The surgeon scowled but didn't reply.

"Are there enough hunters?" Corban asked. "It's one of the smallest guilds."

"We would need to recruit all of them, including former guild members," Derek said.

Corban felt a chill. "I'm willing to help, but please don't expect all the former hunters to volunteer. Robin Aziz has a new baby, and my brother—well, you're aware of his limitations. My idea is safer—shoot them from the sentry lofts."

"Robin is exempt," Derek said, "but Thane will have to decide for himself. Shooting the night terrors from the sentry lofts might take care of the immediate threat, but the cubs left behind in the dens will grow to be more dangerous. We need to wipe them all out." Derek appeared as uncomfortable as Corban felt. "We need trained hunters, no matter how long they've been out of the guild."

"I think we should call for a vote." Solona stood with care, still favoring the healing gunshot wound in her right thigh, and waited until side conversations ceased. "All in favor of sending the hunters to eradicate the night terrors?"

Every hand except Corban's and Dr. DeKalb's was in the air. Corban figured he wasn't allowed to vote with the leaders, although he wouldn't have raised his hand anyway.

Solona turned to her son-in-law, her expression somber. "Motion passes. We'll leave the planning to you and the Hunters Guild master." She nodded to Matteo Evans, who was wearing a sour expression. "Are you in agreement?"

The graying, grizzled, pot-bellied Evans nodded, his expression reminiscent of someone who'd spent too much of his life battling night terrors. "I don't suppose there were any explosives salvaged from the *Unity*'s supplies? We'll need some for this hunt."

"Sorry, no, but assume all colony firearms are at your disposal. Let's adjourn," Solona said. "Thank you for coming. Derek, please keep us apprised on plans for the hunt."

The overhead lights in the room flickered. Corban took it as an ominous sign, but no one else seemed to notice.

Derek moved across the room to confer with Matteo Evans. Neither man seemed enthused at the prospect of organizing a night terror hunt.

Corban exited the south wall corner apartment after Solona. "Thanks for letting me sit in." He fell into step beside her as they headed down the hallway toward the stairwell.

Solona gave him a sympathetic smile. "I'd be lying if I said I wanted you and Thane to join the hunt. Nikki would never forgive me if anything happened to you."

"I'd be lying if I said I don't mind hunting night terrors," Corban said, "but we have to think of the safety of the entire colony."

"I know. I admire your courage for being willing to help."

Corban was surprised to hear this. He thought of Nikki's mother as the most courageous person he knew, next to Thane. Before he thought of a response, she changed the subject.

"Are you ready to sit for the apprenticeship exam?"

"I think so. I've been studying for months, and I've had plenty of hands-on experience at the apothecary."

"Good, because I think you should skip it and take the assistant's exam with Nikki and Jing instead."

Corban gaped at her. "Skip the apprenticeship level? Aren't we too young to be assistants?"

"Imposing age limits was Kun's idea. I'm guild master now, and I think age has nothing to do with competency," Solona said. "You three have been running the Lakeside apothecary without supervision for three months, and it's doing better than the shops at the other forts. The Herbalists Guild needs skilled workers, which is why I've also invited Zhao and Isaac to be in charge of Brida's apothecary."

"I'm sure they'll be glad to return to their guild." Corban grinned. "With Thane and Rupert back in the Smiths Guild, that leaves zero night sentries at West Fort. I guess that's why Mayor Piroux glared at me."

"I informed Guild Master Yarborough last week, and she's already recruiting Strays to replace the communications team."

"You've been busy." Corban was always impressed with Solona's ability to cut through any bureaucratic roadblocks and get things done. "Who else have you pressured lately?"

She smirked but didn't correct him. "I might have mentioned to Bertram that Thane should be moved up to assistant metal-smith."

"Might have mentioned?" Corban echoed.

"That slime worm Rajamani kept Thane from being promoted." Solona paused at the top of the stairs and turned to face Corban. "This colony can't afford to be held back by bigots any longer. Survivors need to accept the fact that the Strays are the hope for Vesta's survival. They owe you respect, not discrimination."

"Attitudes are slow to change." Corban experienced a flutter of fear as he wondered if Solona was going to ask him about his willingness to help add to the population—with Nikki.

Solona gave him a shrewd look but said, "I think the *Unity*'s explosion humbled most of the Survivors."

Corban breathed a mental sigh of relief that no awkward questions were forthcoming. Guild Master Zegarelli had no reservations about being direct, as he discovered every time he spoke with her. He had a feeling he wouldn't be able to avoid awkward questions about his and Nikki's relationship much longer, but thankfully there weren't any potential questions today since Solona seemed to be in a hurry.

"I have to inspect the apothecary here, and I'm sure they won't be happy to see me after I pointed out how inadequate their inventory was last month. I'll see you later, Corban."

"Goodbye, and thank you for everything you've done for Thane and me."

"You're welcome." Solona hurried down the stairs ahead of him and was crossing Main Street into Waterfall's marketplace before Corban emerged from the stairwell.

At eight-hundred by six-hundred meters, Waterfall was twice the size of the other five established forts and four times the size of Brida. The cobblestone streets were laid out in a grid pattern, with an open-air market and row houses filling the courtyard space. Three-story apartment buildings formed the exterior stone walls. Corban turned onto Main Street and walked past the ramp leading underground to the colony's fleet warehouse where the electric vehicles were recharged overnight.

Though it was tempting to ask a mechanic if a truck was available, Corban didn't have a guild master's permission to use one. Officially, the trucks were to be used for transporting goods between forts, although

Corban knew his uncle Leighton had taken advantage of his position as West Fort's mayor to acquire a vehicle for personal use.

He exited Waterfall's main gates and walked across the hydroelectric dam. He paused in the bridge's center to rest his arms on the railing and look down at the waterfall. The wall of concrete, which comprised the dam, was cracked in a few places, but Corban thought that was normal for a structure which had endured forty or more of Vesta's punishing annual storms. The colony harnessed the Cold River's natural fifty-meter plunge, providing enough electricity to light Waterfall and recharge the fleet. The other forts ran on solar power.

The main gravel road north followed the river. Corban hiked a kilometer before he heard an aging vehicle straining to make it up the hill behind himself. A faded black Sentries Guild truck pulled up beside him.

"Need a ride?" Zhao Kaczenski was at the wheel, with Isaac Nomura next to him in the cab. "If you're headed to Lakeside, we can take you as far as West Fort." There was a bike and several gray metal shipping boxes with *Unity* stenciled on the lids in the truck bed.

"I'm headed to the apartment. Thane and I are moving to Lakeside today." Corban went around to the passenger's side door and squeezed in next to Isaac. "Who gave you permission to use a truck?"

Zhao nudged the accelerator, and the bald tires spun before finding traction on the loose gravel. "Solona, of course. We're moving out too."

"She told me," Corban said. "Congratulations. You two feel ready to manage Brida's apothecary?"

"I do," Isaac said. "I was an apprentice before the internment. I've hated every minute of sentry duty."

"I'll need some review," Zhao said, "but Solona will

be there to supervise us since she lives in Brida."

"You didn't want to return to the Mechanics Guild?" Corban asked Zhao.

"No. Machines are fine, but plants are my passion."

Speaking of passion. "Did you talk to Thane today?" Corban tried to sound casual since it wasn't his place to tell Zhao about the engagement.

"No, as soon as we got off sentry duty at daybreak, Isaac and I biked to Waterfall to borrow a truck. I did hear about a night terror climbing inside a window during the party last night and that it almost attacked *mei mei.*"

"You heard right," Corban said. "Did you also hear that Linnea Savoy and another telekinetic Stray stopped the beast when it was about a meter from my throat?"

"Yes, it's the only thing people could talk about in Waterfall this morning," Isaac said. "The fleet mechanics were saying Strays have the ability to merge their Talents like Linnea and what's his name?"

"Sergey Gupta," Corban said. "It's a theory so far, but I hope it proves true. If Nikki and I can merge our Talents, other Strays should be able to do the same, especially those with the same Talents."

"There's a lot we don't understand about Talents," Zhao said. "Learning to control mine took discipline and hours of practice."

"How about you?" Corban asked Isaac. "How long did it take you to learn to use your telescopic vision?"

"I'm still learning. I had no idea I could magnify my vision until last week."

"What?" Zhao gawked at him. "I'm your roommate, and you never thought to mention it to me? I thought you could only see distance."

Isaac shrugged. "I didn't think it was worth mentioning. I had a splinter in my foot, but it was too tiny to see. I concentrated on taking a closer look and my skin cells were suddenly the size of paving stones."

Corban was thoughtful. "It's odd how every Stray I know was timid about exploring his or her Talents. Nikki was afraid to touch anyone, even family members. Thane didn't know how far away he could hear until I spent the night up a tree, yelling for him to not come looking for me."

"What were you doing up a tree?" Isaac asked.

"Avoiding night terrors," Corban said. "I was stuck in the tree with the cache of weapons my uncle buried beneath it."

"Ah, that tree," Isaac said. "But why were you outside the fort at night?"

Corban sighed. "I was being an idiot. That was before I knew night terrors could climb." He winced at the resulting laughter and changed the subject. "I just came from an emergency mayors' meeting at Waterfall this morning." For the remainder of the bumpy ride over washed-out gravel roads, Corban explained the plan to cull the night terror packs.

"Sounds like a good way to get killed." Zhao frowned. "Are you sure you want to volunteer?"

"No, but they need experienced hunters."

"You think Thane will volunteer?" Zhao asked. "*Mei mei* won't like that."

Corban frowned. "I don't think Nikki will be happy with me either."

Zhao drove through the gateway arch and parked the truck near the stairwell to the upper floors of the west wall. They grabbed the empty boxes out of the bed and climbed to the third floor.

Isaac took out a key to unlock the door to 30W just

as Thane poked his head out of 30W-B, ten meters down the hall on the right. "I hope you brought some boxes."

Corban walked down to the room he'd shared with his brother for many storms. It was bittersweet to be leaving a place that held so many terrible memories of their uncle Leighton, yet the room had been a refuge from the abuse. Their uncle rarely entered their space, especially after Thane turned eighteen three storms ago.

"Will four boxes be enough?" Corban followed Thane into their simple bedroom and saw the contents of their shared dresser sorted into neat piles on the hardwood floor. "How did you get here?"

"Caught a ride with Dagmar at daybreak. Mayor Piroux was up all night making cinnamon rolls for both forts, and Dagmar wanted to pick up Brida's portion before the breakfast rush."

Corban set a box next to his pile of clothes. "I'm going to miss her cooking."

"Me too." Thane pointed to the three hammocks— the third one had belonged to Rupert. "We should leave those. I assume the Grahams' apartment has real beds."

"I can't believe we get an apartment to ourselves," Corban said, "after living in a single room for five storms."

"I guess we're officially adults." Thane grabbed the pillows from their hammocks.

The brothers worked fast, boxing up their meager possessions of clothes, toiletries, and a few books and machetes.

Corban was stuffing their towels into the top of the

fourth box when Isaac opened the door to the adjoining bedroom that used to be Leighton's. "Done yet?"

"Yes," Thane said.

"We are too." Isaac crossed their room with a filled backpack and set it outside in the hallway.

"Shouldn't we clean for the next occupants?" Corban looked around at the dirt with a pang of guilt.

"I don't know how to clean." Isaac faked an innocent pout.

"Me either." Zhao joined in the conversation from Uncle's doorway. "If we leave now, we'll have time to drive you two to Lakeside."

"Right," Isaac said. "We start work at the apothecary after lunch, so no time to clean."

Corban exchanged a shrug with Thane, and the four young men carried the boxes down to the waiting truck.

"Goodbye, West Fort," Corban said as they drove through the gates, watching as the stone walls disappeared around a bend.

"Goodbye to bad memories," Thane added next to him.

SEVEN
FIRST CULLING

"I heard you need tomorrow off." Bertram Conquist checked Thane's work, extracting the machete blade from the coals with long-handled tongs.

Thane waited for the new guild master to examine the blade before replying. Since Thane was out of practice as a metal-smith, he didn't mind the extra supervision. "Yes, for the night terror hunt."

Bertram flashed the same lopsided grin as his nephew; Bertram and Rupert's late father, Bernard, had been identical twins. Bertram's hair was also flame-red like Rupert's, although the guild master's was flecked with gray. "It's been a long time since you were in the Hunters Guild. I hope you know what you're doing."

"Me too." Thane smothered a spark of anxiety.

"This looks good." Bertram plunged the blade into the water bucket next to Thane's anvil and spoke over the hiss from the steam. "Think you can make four more by the end of the day?"

"I'll do my best." Thane appreciated having a boss who believed encouragement got better results than criticism. He didn't miss Chaim Rajamani, the former

Stray-hating Smiths Guild master who died aboard the *Unity*.

"Rupert told me you can forge swords." Bertram moved back to his own workstation. "Is it true?"

Thane drew the machete from the water and positioned it on his anvil. He picked up his flatter but finished the explanation before he started on the blade. "I've made one sword, and it was for Leighton. It was a birthday gift, back when I cared what he thought of me. Nikki Ramirez has it now, and she knows how to use it."

"How did it come into her possession? I know the slime worm didn't give it to her."

"No, he didn't." Thane chuckled. "It's a long story."

Bertram grinned. "In that case, you can tell me over lunch."

Thane returned the grin and got back to work. He focused on the machete, trying hard not to think about the night terror hunt the next day.

***

Thane was tightening the Velcro straps on his titanium brace when there was a knock at the door.

"I don't need clairvoyance to know who it is." Corban tucked his loaded pistol into the waistband of his jeans as he walked to the door. "Shall I let her in?"

Thane suppressed a sigh with effort. "Yes."

Jing Kaczenski stood on their doorstep, with clenched fists and a trembling lower lip. She stepped across the threshold without a word.

"It's for you." Corban slipped by her into the hallway and pulled the door shut.

Thane took a deep breath to muster his resolve for round three of their argument. "Good morning." He held out his arms to Jing, but she ignored the gesture.

"I don't want you to go." It came out like a hiss, more demanding than pleading.

"Try to understand I'm doing this for you, for the whole colony," Thane said. "Twice now I've almost lost Corban to a night terror. I'm a good hunter, and they need me today."

Jing moved closer and seized his hands. "There are plenty of others who could help with the hunt. You're not equipped—"

Thane lost the tentative hold on his temper. "You don't think I can handle the hunt because of my leg?"

"Yes!" Jing winced and shook her head. "I mean no!"

"You said my injury doesn't make me less of a man. Weren't those your words?"

"It doesn't! But this is different! Even with a gun, you're no match for a pack of night terrors! No one is! This plan is insane!"

Thane tried a different tactic. "Derek and Guild Master Evans have been planning this for a week."

"That's not enough time!" Jing said. "You have no idea how many night terrors are stalking the colony!"

Thane gestured at his rifle on the kitchen table. "We're well armed."

"Going in shooting without knowing how many night terrors are in a lair isn't a winning strategy, and you know it!"

"It's a risk we have to take. No one is safe until we cull the packs."

Jing held up her left hand. "Doesn't this mean anything to you? You promised to spend your life with me, and now you want to throw it away? I can't lose you!"

"I'm not throwing my life away." Thane didn't know how to help her understand. "You won't lose me."

"You don't know that!"

"I can't back out now. They'll think I'm a coward."

"Let them!" Jing roared. "No one who knows you doubts your courage, Thane Abrams!"

"But maybe you doubt my sanity?" Thane pulled his hands free. "You think a cripple shouldn't have to do his part to help the colony?"

"You're not a cripple!"

Thane turned away. "I'll be fine. Corban and I will have each other's backs."

"This is suicide!" Jing sobbed. "Please don't go!"

Thane took a deep breath, frustrated the argument had come full circle. He had real doubts about Jing's maturity at times like this. *But, if I'm being honest with myself, I'd react the same way if she was the one going out to hunt night terrors.*

"I need to do this." Thane slung his backpack over his shoulder. It was heavy with the extra ammunition for his rifle. "I'll use my Talent to avoid unnecessary risks, I promise. The team is waiting for me."

Jing reached into the pocket of her jacket and pulled out a small glass cylinder. She pressed it into his hand. "Take this, please."

Thane opened his palm to examine the little bottle. It was filled with a clear liquid, and the neck was sealed with wax. A narrow strip of fabric passed through the wax like a candle wick. "What is it?"

"You'll need this too." Jing put a striker in his hand with the bottle. "Light the fabric and throw it as far as you can."

"What is it?" Thane repeated.

"It's an explosive device Nikki made. I don't know what it's called. She found the directions in an Earth history datafile." Jing stretched to give him a quick kiss, her face wet with tears. "Try not to get yourself killed." She threw herself into a chair and erupted in fresh sobs.

Thane felt guilty leaving while she was an emotional wreck but knew he'd never escape if he waited for her to calm down and change her mind—since she wouldn't do either. He didn't think Jing meant to be manipulative when she turned on the waterworks, but at times like this, it sure felt that way.

"I'll meet you in the dining hall for dinner," he said with more confidence than he felt. Thane tucked the bottle and striker into the smallest cargo pocket of his jeans and secured the button closure. He grabbed the rifle from the table and stepped outside the apartment, pulling the door shut harder than he intended.

Corban was waiting for him in the hallway, arms folded across his chest and gazing at the ceiling. Thane assumed he'd overheard everything.

"It's not too late to back out," Corban said.

"Don't you start," Thane grumbled.

"Did she give you one of these?" Corban held up a twin of Thane's explosive device before tucking it back into his own cargo pocket.

"Yes. What is it?" Thane headed down the hall toward the door to the courtyard, Corban falling into step beside him.

"I don't know, but I wish Nikki made more. We have no idea how many night terrors are in one lair, and I'd prefer to eliminate the whole pack instead of one at a time."

"That's assuming these actually explode."

Corban raised an eyebrow. "You doubt Nikki's skills? Look who raised her—the woman who saved your fiancée's life. Few people could save themselves with a gunshot wound to the leg, much less rescue another person."

Thane managed a weak nod of agreement. "Maybe Solona should be leading this hunt."

There was a gray Hunters Guild truck parked outside the fortress gates. Since Thane had been a resident of Lakeside for less than a week, he didn't recognize most of the people loading the bed with an assortment of weapons, including crossbows, rifles, machetes, and boxes of ammunition. A few people greeted them, but most of the group was quiet, the atmosphere heavy with tension.

Three people Thane did recognize were sitting in the cab. Derek Graham was at the wheel, with Fenton DeKalb squeezed between him and Isaac Nomura in the passenger's seat. Thane had seen happier faces at a funeral. He nodded to them.

Derek sent a mental message in reply. *I'd rather be doing anything but this. Eliana isn't too happy with me right now.*

Thane raised an eyebrow at the mayor and moved to the back of the truck.

Hunters Guild master Matteo Evans eyed Thane's brace but didn't challenge him. To the group he said, "Let's go."

Thane climbed into the truck bed and sat next to Corban, setting the heavy rifle across his lap. The guild master settled next to him, and Thane wondered if he was in for a lecture on why a cripple shouldn't be hunting night terrors. The other six hunters found seats in the bed. Derek put the vehicle in gear and pulled away from the fort.

Evans outlined the situation. "DeKalb, Nomura, and I scouted the colony boundaries for the past five days. Yesterday DeKalb caught the scent of a cave with a large lair, and Nomura saw the tufts of white fur all over the ground around it." He tilted his head toward the cab, indicating the members of the team who weren't hunters. "It's not far from the stone barn outside Orchard Valley.

"Night terrors breached the barn the night before last. All the sheep and goats were slaughtered." Evans scowled as he attached a scope to the barrel of his rifle. "My stepson was on the Farmers Guild cleanup detail, but he told me nothing could be salvaged."

"Good thing Greenfield keeps the lambs, kids, and nursing mothers in their courtyard, or we'd be out of another source of protein," Corban said.

"And wool." Evans nodded.

Thane stared at Gray Lake as the truck turned south onto the main road. He was startled when Evans addressed him.

"We could use your Talent when we get close to the lair, Abrams. I'm glad you decided to join us."

Thane turned to face the guild master. "Thank you, sir. I'll do what I can."

"DeKalb can tell us where they are, and Nomura will keep watch over the whole area. Graham will be with him to communicate with us. One thing we need to know is if the night terrors are asleep. That's where you come in. If you hear one wake up—"

"Intelligent creatures like night terrors probably post sentries," Corban interrupted. "I doubt they'll all be asleep."

"No one knows what they do during the day," Evans said. "Maybe they come out at night because they have sensitive eyesight."

"No one's been crazy enough to confront them in their lairs until today." Thane absent mindedly stroked the stock of his rifle with one hand.

"We don't know how their lairs are laid out," Evans said, "but if we can surround them, we should be able to take them out."

"So one and done?" Thane asked.

Evans grimaced. "We're not sure how many lairs there are. This is the first one we've identified."

Thane didn't want to risk his life more than once, so he didn't comment. He exchanged a worried frown with his brother.

"I still think we should shoot them from the sentries' catwalks," Corban said. "It'd be much safer."

Evans shook his head. "There'll be cubs in the dens. They'll grow up and continue to threaten the colony. Night terrors aren't like Earth bears or wolves. We have no idea how their social order works. Maybe they never sleep. We know how sharp their sense of smell is though."

"That's why hunting them during the day is so dangerous," Corban said. "They might be able to smell us in their sleep."

"Let's stop speculating." Thane's anxiety was growing. "We've got a job to do." He leaned close to whisper to Corban. "Any premonitions about today?"

"No." Corban gnawed his lower lip. "Nothing."

"I hope it means we'll all survive."

***

Derek parked next to the stone barn where three more Hunters Guild trucks were waiting. Everyone piled out of the vehicles and armed themselves, organizing their weapons.

Thane noted the breach in the barn's foundation. A ragged hole had been excavated beneath the stones by what appeared to be hundreds of claw marks. There were blood-stains and tufts of fur and wool covering the ground in every direction.

"Hopefully they'll be sleeping off the recent feast." The optimism in Evans's tone didn't match his frown. He walked among the twenty men and women for a few minutes, inspecting their weapons and offering advice.

Thane filled his large cargo pocket with three spare magazines for his rifle. Despite the day being a few degrees cooler than normal, he was drenched with perspiration.

"Are you a good shot?" Evans took the rifle from him and peered through the scope before handing it back.

"Good enough," Thane replied. "I'll take this over a machete any day."

Evans grunted and moved on to Corban, who handed the older man his pistol. "I can't manage a big rifle or a machete since I was shot four months ago," Corban said. "I don't have the strength on my right side anymore."

"This will get the job done." Evans offered him a rare smile.

Isaac approached Thane. "Derek and I will be up on the roof of the barn."

"I wish I could sit this out on the roof." Fenton DeKalb leaned against the tailgate. Thane thought he seemed paler than normal.

"Abrams?" Evans waited until both brothers faced him. "You two flank DeKalb as he leads the way. Keep him safe."

"Yes, sir," Thane said.

Fenton moved to stand beside Thane and Corban,

hesitation in every step. Dr. Lorna DeKalb's son was thirty but still single. The dark-haired Carpenters Guild partner was tall and muscular, the opposite of his tiny, petite mother. Thane suspected that Fenton agreed to help with the hunt because he was a member of Fort Brida's community council and expected to demonstrate leadership qualities. It was obvious the man was terrified and would rather be building furniture back in his workshop.

"You all right?" Corban asked Fenton.

Fenton patted the handgun holstered at his waist. "Evans gave me fifteen minutes to practice with this. I'll be fine."

Thane didn't crack a smile at his sarcasm. "We'll make sure nothing gets close enough so you need to use it."

Fenton looked doubtful but didn't reply.

"Is everyone ready?" Evans didn't wait for answers before announcing, "Move out."

The hunters fell into formation behind Corban, Thane, and Fenton as the latter led them away from the orchards surrounding the barn to a rocky field on the other side of the road. Massive stones and storm-damaged trees dotted the landscape. Each man or woman spread out, rifles or bows ready to fire as they stepped cautiously across the uneven ground. The group moved in near-silence, navigating fallen branches, stones, night terror scat, and the remains of sheep and goats, their entrails and mauled carcasses scattered everywhere.

Thane was grateful he hadn't eaten breakfast. He imagined the stench was a brutal assault on Fenton's enhanced sense of smell. He protected the carpenter's right, walking a few steps behind him, moving as fast as he could with his bad leg, but since the entire group was proceeding with care, he didn't have to worry about falling behind. Thane wondered if Evans put him in the front with Fenton to set the pace for the group and felt a flicker of gratitude for the thoughtful gesture.

Corban was two steps ahead of Fenton, covering his left. With a warning frown, he glanced back over his shoulder at Thane.

"What?" Thane mouthed the word.

"Something's wrong," Corban murmured. "We shouldn't be here."

"You're telling me this now?" Thane hissed, his heart pounding against his ribs. He looked around at the other hunters and knew it was too late to retreat.

Fenton stopped and pointed to a rock formation ahead. It appeared to be a natural underground bunker with several entrances. "The smell is overwhelming. I can't go any closer," he whispered.

Corban paused too and held up his right fist as a signal to the other hunters. He raised an index finger and rotated his arm. The guild got the message to fan out and surround the cave.

Thane moved closer to Fenton and focused his Talent. He heard night terrors breathing, so many that it was difficult to estimate their numbers. An occasional soft yip indicated the presence of cubs. A thought crossed his mind that night terror mothers would do anything to protect their young, as if the beasts needed another reason to attack humans. *This is insane, like Jing said.*

"Can you climb trees?" Corban whispered on Fenton's other side.

Thane opened his eyes, noted his brother's fearful expression, and grabbed Fenton's elbow. "Over there."

He nodded toward a leaning hardwood tree eight meters to their right.

Fenton nodded, and the three men moved to the tree without a sound.

The night terrors were waking up. Instead of deep breathing, Thane heard low-pitched growls, which were gradually increasing in volume, but he had no way to warn the other hunters.

Reaching the tree, Thane got down on his good knee, set his rifle on the ground, and laced his fingers together to give Fenton a foothold. The carpenter gripped Thane's shoulders, set a foot in his hands, and reached up as Thane stood, lifting him to the lowest hanging limb. Fenton needed no encouragement to climb higher.

Thane knelt again and offered Corban the foothold.

Corban shook his head. "You go first."

"You're not strong enough to lift me, and we don't have time to argue."

"I'm not leaving you unprotected."

"You can cover me while I climb up."

"You two might want to hurry," Fenton called. "The smell's getting stronger."

"So's the noise." Thane's mouth went dry. "They're awake."

Fenton waved frantically to get Evans's attention, but it was too late. The quiet was broken by the crazed barking and snarls of night terrors.

Here they come! Derek warned.

The beasts exploded from the cave, fanning out to attack the hunters from all sides. Gunshots rang out, the hunters drilling the beasts with bullets and arrows, cutting down the first wave.

There's more! Derek thought. *Twice as many!*

Corban set his foot in Thane's hands and hoisted

himself into the tree. "Get up here!"

Thane jumped as high as he could, but his good leg was unable to find purchase on the slick bark.

Corban gripped a branch with his legs and reached down to where Thane could almost grab his hand. "Come on!"

Thane heard a piercing scream above the staccato of gunshots and barking but was unable to look away from the night terrors bearing down on him.

EIGHT
OUTNUMBERED

Three night terrors broke from the main pack and raced toward the tree. One of the monsters had an arrow sticking out of its back, but that didn't appear to slow its speed.

"Thane!" Corban reached lower. He regretted climbing up first. Now he had no way to help his brother to safety.

Fenton fumbled out his pistol and shot at the approaching creatures, killing the one with the arrow. It collapsed in the dirt, but its companions didn't break stride.

Thane brought up his rifle and aimed at the lead beast, shooting it in the head, but the one behind it dodged the body and kept coming.

Corban reacted without thinking, swinging his legs around the limb and dropping to the ground next to Thane.

"What are you doing?" Thane's voice cracked. "Get back up there!"

Corban drew his pistol and unloaded all six shots into the night terror closing in on them. Ten meters, five. It was slowing, but he and Thane started running, desperate to put more space between themselves and the beast.

Thane brought his rifle up and turned around to take another shot. The monster snarled, spraying them with blood-tinged saliva, and rose onto its hind legs, displaying paws the size of frying pans crowned with razor-sharp claws.

The creature was massive, larger than any night terror Corban had ever seen. It was gushing blood from multiple gunshot wounds in its back and neck, yet it continued to move forward, determined to reach them.

Fenton and Thane fired again. Fenton's shot went through the top of its skull, and Thane's pierced its left eye. The night terror gave a howl of outrage and finally came to a halt. It fell forward onto its bloody snout, missing Corban's feet by a decimeter.

"Darkness." Corban's hands were shaking as he loaded his pistol with a fresh magazine. He turned to Thane, who was white-faced and trembling. "That was too close."

Evans is in trouble! Derek warned.

Corban looked around at the battle raging across the field. None of the hunters had a moment to rest as they fired bullets and arrows into the attacking night terrors, trying to stay clear of their deadly jaws. Dozens of large white bodies blended in with the field stones, but more night terrors were emerging from the cave, ready to relieve their fallen comrades.

"Over there!" Thane pointed to a cluster of tall rocks twenty meters to their left. "Evans is behind those! He's surrounded!"

"Don't move!" Corban bellowed to Fenton.

"Of course not!" Fenton gripped the tree trunk

with both hands. "Be careful!"

Thane took off in his odd skipping run, and Corban raced after him.

Corban's stomach gave a lurch as he almost tripped over the body of a fallen hunter, a woman. She was face down so he couldn't see who it was. There was a pool of blood beneath her head, evidence that a night terror found her throat. He swallowed the bile rising in his own throat and focused on reaching Guild Master Evans.

A horrible scream cut through the din of gunshots and snarls. It was a man's scream of pain or horror, or both. Corban raced past Thane and reached the rocks first, his pistol ready as he tore around to the other side.

Matteo Evans's back was against a boulder, and he was slashing at the muzzle of a night terror with a small hunting knife, his rifle on the ground out of reach. The beast's jaws were around Evans's left thigh, pinning him against the rock. Corban shot the beast in the back, and it turned around to face him, dragging Evans with it.

The guild master screamed again as he was flung to the ground, his leg a fountain of bright red blood gushing from the monster's jaws.

"Darkness." Thane gasped behind Corban.

They shot the night terror several times, taking care not to hit Evans, until at last the creature released his leg and slumped over dead.

Two more night terrors approached Evans, but Corban fired quickly, eliminating the threat.

More headed your way! Derek thought.

"Make a tourniquet." Corban whipped off his belt and tossed it at Thane. "And give me your bottle." He drew the explosive device and striker from his cargo pocket.

"What're you going to do?" Thane handed his bottle to Corban before kneeling next to Evans. He looped Corban's belt above the guild master's ruined thigh below his pelvis.

"I'm going to destroy the lair." A strange calm filled Corban, sharpening his focus. "It's time to end this."

"No!" Thane cinched the belt tight to stanch the bleeding. "Sorry," he murmured to Evans, who was groaning in pain. Thane shouted over his shoulder at Corban, "You won't be able to get close enough! There's too many!"

"I can throw with my left arm." Corban clicked open his striker and lit the fabric strip on one of the bottles.

"Don't light it until you're ready!"

Corban realized his mistake before Thane shouted the warning. He raced around to the other side of the rocks. With no time to analyze the distance, he launched the bottle in the direction of the lair thirty meters away. He covered his ears and turned his face away before the projectile hit the ground ten meters short of the goal.

The bottle bomb exploded, sending up a geyser of flame, earth, and debris, and taking out a pair of night terrors.

Darkness, that was intense. The fire died fast, leaving behind a cloud of black smoke over the fresh crater. Corban scanned the field to make sure the other hunters were clear of the den before running toward it, determined to get close enough to do real damage with the second bottle.

Night terrors approaching on your left! Corban dismissed Derek's mental warning. He needed both hands free to light the bottle bomb, so his pistol remained tucked into his waistband.

Four beasts stood in front of the largest entrance to the lair, and Corban knew he'd be surrounded if he got any closer. He ran up a large boulder, lit the second bottle, and threw it. He dropped to the ground and covered his head with his arms this time.

The explosion was followed by a shower of pebbles and debris raining down on everything in the vicinity. Corban waited until the fallout stopped before climbing to his feet and drawing his gun.

The night terrors attacking from his left paused, their snarls quieting to whimpers of confusion as they stared past him to the smoke drifting over the rubble from the cave. Corban took advantage of their hesitation to shoot each one in the skull, dropping them easily. He suspected adrenaline aided his accuracy. He faced the lair again and surveyed the bodies of night terrors sprawled around it. There wasn't much left of the four at the entrance.

What were those bombs you used, and do you have any more? Relief was evident in Derek's tone.

Corban turned toward the stone barn and shook his head, assuming Isaac would see the gesture with his enhanced vision. He took a moment to get his bearings, aware of the sudden silence. No barking or snarling, no more gunshots. He rotated a full circle, searching for night terrors, but didn't see any standing. *Is that it? It's over?*

Fenton waved to him from his treetop perch. There were three dead beasts lying at the base of the trunk. Corban gave Fenton a half-hearted thumbs-up and made a mental note to congratulate him later on his marksmanship.

He loaded his pistol with a fresh magazine before hurrying back to Thane and Evans. Corban found his brother sitting on the ground, face in his blood-covered hands, beside the prostate guild master. Evans wasn't moving.

"He lost too much blood." Thane's voice was filled with anguish. "The tourniquet wasn't enough. I couldn't get the bleeding to stop."

Corban sat next to Thane and put a firm hand on his shaking shoulder. "There wasn't anything else you could do." He glanced at Evans's leg and looked away before his stomach turned over. "It must have bitten through his femoral artery." He reached over to close Evans's vacant eyes.

"Come on." Corban stood and pulled Thane to his feet. "Let's check on the others."

"Who was on the ground?" Thane asked. "The person we stepped over?"

"I don't know." Corban hoped it wasn't anyone they knew.

"Jing was right." Thane's voice was soft as he followed Corban across the battlefield. "One week wasn't enough time to plan the hunt. If it wasn't for the bottle bombs, we might both be dead."

Corban's adrenaline was ebbing, leaving him exhausted and shaky. He tamped down on the urge to snap at Thane. "Please don't talk about the what-if's right now. Let's just see who needs help."

"I guess it's too late to help her." Thane's tone turned frosty, but Corban didn't have the emotional energy to spare for a rebuttal.

They reached the fallen huntress and crouched on either side of her without a word. Working together, they turned her over. Corban instantly wished they hadn't. Thane turned away from the woman's face, which was mauled beyond recognition, and vomited into the weeds. Corban struggled to hold back the gorge rising in his throat and found that shutting his eyes was the only thing that helped. He stripped off his T-shirt and covered the woman's ruined face and neck.

"Who was she?" Thane wiped his mouth on the hem of his own T-shirt.

"I don't know." Corban stood and turned away from the huntress. "Come on. We need to go. The hunt's over. Derek can message the mortician to recover the bodies."

"Did we do it? Did we kill the pack?" Thane stood shakily, his face as white as a night terror's fur.

"I think we eliminated this one." Corban saw the other hunters heading toward the stone barn. He put an arm around Thane's shoulders and urged him to start walking. Corban lost count of how many night terror bodies were scattered across the field. He didn't envy whomever the mayors assigned to bury the carcasses. *They'll need the backhoe.*

Fenton climbed down from the tree and fell into step beside them. "Darkness, what a stench."

"You don't need a Talent to notice," Thane said.

"I feel like I'm waking up from a nightmare," Fenton said.

"This was only the first lair," Corban said. "The nightmare's just begun."

NINE
CORBAN'S SECRET

"Shh, don't move." Nikki stood in front of Corban and gripped his shoulders. She shut her eyes as his memories crowded her mind. She focused her Talent, sifting through the images, searching. His mind was busy, a churning whirlpool of emotions, and it was taking too long to locate the one she needed to see. "Just show me." The request came out harsher than she intended.

I'll try. His tone was contrite; she knew he sensed her anger.

Nikki struggled to neutralize her own emotions. Her temper was getting in the way, creating a dark, hazy connection she'd never experienced before with Corban.

Sorry. She loosened her grip on his shoulders and leaned in to brush his lips with a gentle kiss. The gesture helped dispel the darkness.

The light filtered in, displacing the anger and soothing her nerves. It allowed her to focus on Corban's memory of the ill-fated hunt he'd returned from an hour ago. She watched it from the beginning, like a horror holo-vid set on fast-forward. She flinched at the sight of the huge night terror on its hind legs, at Evans's ruined leg, at the dead huntress with the mangled face.

You were so brave. She scanned backward for a few images and watched him throw the bottle bomb again, destroying the lair.

I couldn't have done it without your help. Those explosives saved our lives.

Nikki opened her eyes and peered into Corban's freshly washed face, his hair damp from the recent shower. *Was culling the night terrors a success? Please tell me there'll be no more hunts.*

This was only the first lair.

She studied his brown eyes, centimeters from her own, and decided her questions could wait. He'd endured enough for one day. "You should go back to your apartment and get some rest. See you at dinner?"

Corban nodded, kissed her on the cheek, and left the apothecary.

***

Dinner in the dining hall was a somber occasion. Nikki pushed the food around her plate with a fork, separating the grilled chicken from the corn, beans, and quinoa, then mixing it together into an unappetizing mess. She peered across the table at Thane and Jing, who'd spent the afternoon arguing. Nikki had been a reluctant bystander, overhearing through the closed door of the apothecary examination room, since they didn't bother keeping their voices down. Nothing was resolved because neither would budge from his or her position. Now they sat in stony silence, not looking at each other and not eating. Nikki had strong doubts about their compatibility as a couple.

"Sorry I'm late." Corban slipped into the chair next to Nikki's and set his half-empty plate on the table. "What'd I miss?"

"Just uncomfortable silence." Jing peered sideways at Thane. "We've agreed not to talk about the hunt over dinner."

"Don't want to spoil our appetites." Thane's tone dripped with sarcasm. He pushed away his untouched plate and studied the tabletop with a frustrated scowl.

Corban found Nikki's hand under the table. *Chilly in here.*

Like a meat locker, she thought.

"The bottle bombs you two gave us were a big help, but I don't think an arsenal of those will be enough." Corban squeezed Nikki's hand. *I'll need your support for what I'm about to say.* "I think I have a solution for the next hunt."

"There isn't going to be a next hunt—!" Jing flared up at once.

Nikki snapped, "Let him finish!"

"Thank you." Corban took a deep breath. "Derek messaged me about another mayors' meeting tomorrow. I'm going to attend and recommend that the Strays help with the next hunt."

"That's a terrible idea!" Jing said.

Nikki shot her a quelling look, and Jing harrumphed and leaned back in her chair. "Please continue," Nikki said to Corban.

"I think the solution is in merging our Talents."

Thane brought his chin up, showing interest in the discussion for the first time.

"If Linnea and Sergey were able to freeze a night terror in mid-pounce, there must be other Talents that could make a hunt safer for everyone."

"We know so little about merging," Nikki said. "Have Linnea and Sergey been able to duplicate what they did at the reception? I mean, with something other than a night terror?"

"I don't know," Corban said.

"If three or more telekinetics worked together, could they move something larger?" Thane asked.

"I'm sure Solona's focused on this since the reception," Corban said. "It might take months to test Strays and see if they can merge their Talents. The possibilities are daunting."

"The possibilities are endless." Thane turned his head to give Jing a half-smile. "What if another Stray with a hearing Talent worked with me? Maybe by merging our Talents, we could hear farther than two kilometers."

"Maybe, next hunt, you could sit on the roof with Derek to warn the hunters *before* the beasts attack," Corban said. "Your Talent was wasted walking right up to the lair since you couldn't warn the other hunters."

Jing spoke in a husky voice. "There are plenty of ways to help the colony without risking your life."

Thane locked eyes with Corban. Nikki could almost see the wheels turning in Thane's mind.

I believe Mr. Stubborn is about to concede, Corban thought. *I wish he'd done it hours ago.*

"I agree." Thane seemed to have a difficult time getting the words out, but he turned to study Jing's profile, his expression hopeful. "I won't participate in the next hunt except from a safe distance."

Nikki thought Thane was the most patient man she'd ever met. She wondered how much Jing would test his patience, assuming they still wanted to marry.

Are you kidding? Corban thought. *He'd walk over hot coals in his bare feet if she asked him to.*

Nikki giggled.

"What's so funny?" Jing's eyes flicked back and forth between them. "Would you two please not do that mind-reading thing when we're trying to have a discussion?"

"Is that what we're doing?" Thane raised his eyebrows at Jing. "We're done arguing?"

As Nikki suspected, Jing couldn't continue with the blustery attitude. She was already getting teary-eyed.

"I'm sorry I shouted at you, but I've never felt so scared. You could've been killed today." Jing covered her face with her hands.

"But I wasn't." Thane put an arm around her shoulders. Jing didn't resist.

"Two people were killed," Corban said. "It was chaos. I never would've volunteered if I knew we'd be outnumbered ten to one."

"Sounds like a premonition would've come in handy." Thane rose from his chair. "Come on, angel, I'll walk you home."

Jing sniffled and allowed him to help her to her feet. "Don't call me that. I'm no angel."

Thane seemed to be trying hard not to smile. "What would you like me to call you?"

Your Majesty? Corban thought.

Nikki snorted with laughter, earning a warning scowl from Jing.

"I'm sure you'll think of something." She flashed Thane an all-is-forgiven smile, and they exited the dining hall together.

Nikki and Corban sat in silence for a few minutes. She appreciated how their shared light dispelled the tension she'd endured all afternoon. *It's a shame Thane doesn't have access to something like this.*

Thane can handle Jing's mood swings. Compared to Uncle, Jing's drama is a pleasant holiday.

Ugh. Let's not spoil the mood by discussing your uncle—or the hunt—unless you need to talk about it?

No, but I need your help composing a speech to the mayors about allowing the Strays to help with future hunts.

She lifted her cup with her free hand and took a sip of water. *Let's approach Mom first. She knows how to handle the mayors.* As Nikki's tension faded, her appetite grew. *I'm getting a new plate from the buffet.*

Corban smiled. *Good idea.*

They filled plates from the long table set with platters of poached fish, grilled chicken and purple crawler, assorted salads, baked sweet potatoes, black beans, corn, quinoa, and slices of bread that Corban declared, "Almost edible, if you smother it with jam."

"Every fort can't have a baking expert like Mayor Piroux in the kitchen." Nikki refilled her water cup, and they returned to the table.

The dinner rush was over. A few couples and groups of friends lingered at half a dozen tables around the room. Nikki and Corban sat across from each other and talked about everything except night terrors while they ate. She was beginning to relax when he said something odd.

"I could picture us doing this every night." He grimaced as if it had slipped out and looked down at his plate.

Nikki wasn't sure how to respond. "You mean eating together? Right here, in the dining hall?"

Corban's cheeks took on a rosy hue. "No, not exactly." He seemed to have something on his mind, and it wasn't difficult to guess what.

"Did you have a premonition?" She waited until his eyes met hers. "About us?"

He nodded.

"Was it bad?" She mustered a teasing grin. "Was I coming at you with the sword again?"

"It wasn't bad." He hesitated. "But it takes place so far into the future that I didn't want to tell you. It might put too much pressure on our relationship."

"Really?" Nikki realized he was right. *Would it be better not knowing?* "How do you handle the stress of knowing the future? You have to live with it every day."

"I can't stop the premonitions, and half the time I can't figure out what they mean, so I push them to the back of my mind. Until I have another one," he added with a sigh.

"I'm guessing you haven't been able to stop thinking about this one? Is there a reason you don't want to tell me about it?" Nikki reached across the table for his hand, but he moved it to his lap with an apologetic frown. "How long ago did you have this dream?"

"The night you were stuck in the library, hiding from the *Unity*'s crew."

"Hiding because I sent my father to the hospital ship." Nikki pursed her lips, thinking. "That was over a month ago, and you didn't want to tell me?"

He shook his head. "I wasn't sure you'd want to know about this one."

"You've done a good job hiding it from me."

Corban closed his eyes. "I'm trying to decide if you should see my memory or if I should just describe it to you."

She frowned. "Were you planning to leave some details out of your description?"

"No." He puffed out his cheeks and exhaled a long breath. "I think a description would minimize the shock."

Nikki's mouth fell open. "I think I need to see it."

Corban wrinkled his brow. "You're sure?"

She left her hand on the table, waiting for him to take it. "Focus on the premonition."

"You can't go back to blissful ignorance once you've seen it."

He's worried about this! Nikki hesitated. "I don't want to spend my time wondering. You've piqued my interest. I think it would be better to take the risk." She gave him a sympathetic smile. "You don't have to carry this burden alone."

"I thought it might be better keeping this to myself, but it's gnawed at me for weeks." Corban extended his hand. "Don't say I didn't warn you."

Nikki shut her eyes, grasped his sweaty palm, and Corban's memory filled her mind.

He was in Lakeside's infirmary, where he'd spent several days recovering from a fever, but this time he wasn't the patient. He was standing at the foot of his bed in front of the narrow window, but someone else was lying in it, sound asleep. None of the other beds were occupied. It was late, and the room was dark, illuminated by weak starlight through the single windowpane. He thought about turning on a lamp, but something made him hesitate. He had a feeling he shouldn't wake the patient.

He sensed peace and contentment, but it took him a few moments to realize those feelings weren't emanating from the patient. There was something warm cradled in his arms. He looked down and gasped. He was holding a newborn baby bundled in a soft blanket. All Corban saw in the poor lighting was a tiny face looking up at his with great interest.

Corban tore his gaze from the infant's bright eyes and moved around to the side of the bed to take a closer look at the patient.

At this point, Nikki gasped aloud. She'd already guessed who Corban was about to discover, but she struggled to stay focused on the memory. She needed to know.

She saw herself lying on her side, her long black hair splayed across the pillow. She looked exhausted.

Of course I'm exhausted! I just had a baby!

The real-life Corban sitting across from her squeezed her hand. *Yes, I'm holding our child.*

Nikki's eyes popped open, and she snatched her hand from his grasp.

"I told you, you might not want to know." His shoulders drooped. "I'm sorry."

"I need time," she stammered, trying to catch her breath, "time to process." Nikki resisted the urge to bolt from the table and race back to her apartment. "We look older. It was so dark it was hard to see, but I think we're older. This won't happen for many storms."

"I hope so," Corban said. "I'm not ready."

"*You think I am?*" Nikki didn't mean to screech the words. She was aware of curious faces turning their way and lowered her voice. "Sorry. It's just . . . a lot to think about."

"It was easier when I was the only one thinking about it." Corban touched her knee under the table. *Let's push it to the back of our minds and try not to dwell on it.*

It will take time for me to do that, if I ever do. Nikki pushed her chair back and got to her feet. "I should go."

Corban popped up from his seat. "I'll walk you home."

"No, I need to be alone. I need time to think." She spun on her heel and headed to the door. "See you at work," she said over her shoulder.

"Goodnight, Nikki." He sounded surprised and a little hurt.

What did he expect? He dropped a bottle bomb on me and tells me I should just forget about it?

Darkness. A baby, with Corban. Nikki didn't want to think about shouldering such a heavy responsibility, not when she was only eighteen storms. She'd watched her older sister deliver Travis and observed Eliana's struggles as a new mother—the sleepless nights, the colic, the constant worry. *Maybe in five storms I'll be ready to* think *about it, but not now.*

Nikki made it to the second floor of the south wall in record time. She was a few doors away from 26S when she realized Thane and Jing might be preoccupied.

"Thane, I'm twenty meters from the apartment. I need you to go home now. I need to be alone, so tell Jing not to pout about it." She slowed her steps until she stopped at the door and counted to ten in her mind before reaching for the doorknob.

Thane opened the door before she did. He was pink in the face and slightly out of breath. "I was just leaving. Goodnight, Nikki." He grinned over his shoulder at Jing, whose face was glowing red like Ilios setting. "See you tomorrow, *meili.*"

"I love you!" Jing called after him.

Nikki shut the door. "What does *meili* mean? Doesn't Zhao call you *mei mei*? Is it the same thing?"

"*Mei mei* means little sister, and I don't want Thane calling me that." Jing giggled. "*Meili* means beautiful in Mandarin."

Nikki made an effort not to roll her eyes. "You two should set a date soon. Preferably *before* you start making babies."

Jing didn't seem to hear. "I'm relieved he won't volunteer for any more hunts except to use his Talent from a safe distance."

"I'm happy for you." Nikki wasn't able to muster the enthusiasm to sound sincere, so she headed to the bathroom. "I'm going to bed."

Jing was right on her heels. "Is Corban going to help with the next hunt?"

"He didn't say." Nikki tried to close the door, but Jing stuck her foot in the way.

"Aren't you scared he'll get hurt or killed? You can't let him hunt again. It's suicide."

"It's none of my business if Corban volunteers for the next hunt," Nikki said. "Excuse me." She nudged Jing's foot out of the way and shut the door in her face.

"Of course it's your business." Jing continued the conversation through the door.

Nikki turned on the water at the sink. "I can't hear you."

Jing increased her volume. "You said you love him, so that makes his life your business."

"I don't want to talk about this right now." Nikki set her jaw. "Please leave me alone."

"If Corban's anything like his brother, he's just being stubborn. You have to persuade him to see reason." Jing was almost shouting.

Nikki slammed her fists on the counter. "He's nothing like Thane! I'm not his mother, and you shouldn't try to be Thane's! He's a grown man and can make his own decisions!"

Jing made a clucking sound. "All right, don't burst a blood vessel. I'm only trying to help."

Nikki glimpsed her red face in the mirror and shut off the water. "I don't need your help with Corban. Please leave me alone."

"Did you two have a fight?" Jing persisted.

Nikki stepped to the shower and turned the water on full blast. "Goodnight!"

TEN
VOLUNTEER

Corban slept badly. Although Nikki's reaction to the baby premonition was less emotional than he'd expected, her abrupt departure troubled him. He was unable to concentrate on a speech for the mayors and was bleary eyed, tense, and unprepared for the early morning meeting. He didn't know how to convince the group of colony leaders that the Strays were their best option for culling the night terrors, especially since merging Talents hadn't been tested.

He was relieved to see Solona in attendance as he slipped inside the Waterfall community council room a few minutes after the meeting had started. She sat at the head of the table again with the seven mayors filling the other seats. This time one guild master was in attendance besides Solona: Athena Yarborough, head of the sentries. Derek Graham appeared downcast, having witnessed the disastrous hunt that claimed the life of his friend Evans and the huntress whose identity Corban didn't know.

Corban needed a few minutes to discuss his proposal with Solona before the meeting, but since he was late, he sat in an empty chair behind her and tried to organize his thoughts.

"We all know the hunt was a tragedy," Derek was saying. "We had no idea there were so many night terrors. If it weren't for two bottle bombs the Abrams brothers provided—"

"They're called Molotov cocktails," Solona interrupted. "Nikki made them."

Derek continued without missing a beat. "If it weren't for the Molotov cocktails, we would've lost more than Evans and his daughter Oksana."

Corban grimaced. *Darkness. Two members of the same family?*

"The question is," Mayor Gina Piroux said, "what can we do to ensure the next hunt is safer? Night terrors can obviously see in the daylight but choose to hunt at night, so we're fortunate they haven't changed their routine. It makes me nervous to think we're not safe outside the forts during the day."

"They came out because we forced them," Derek said. "We got close to their lair, and they were defending themselves. It's their acute sense of smell that makes them dangerous predators, not their vision."

Mayor Piroux shook her head. "The point is we can't risk more lives going after the beasts without a better plan in place."

"Agreed," Derek said, "which is why I recommend accepting Corban Abrams's suggestion to shoot them from the sentry catwalks before we plan another daytime hunt."

Corban stared at Derek in amazement, but the Fort Brida mayor didn't send him any messages.

Several side conversations arose as the other mayors considered Derek's proposal. Corban wondered when to speak up.

"Vesta needs to replace the Hunters Guild master before we can think about planning another hunt," Mayor Pavitra Brooks said. "It's too dangerous to attempt without experienced leadership."

"Who was next in line for guild master?" Yarborough asked.

"Oksana Evans." Derek frowned.

There were mutters of concern, but Solona took charge of the meeting again. "It's up to this group to decide how to proceed until the hunters elect a new leader. I suggest the sentries cull as many beasts as they can tonight and tomorrow night, then send Guild Master Yarborough an estimate of how many remain on third night."

"Most sentries are armed with staffs," Yarborough said, "so we'll need volunteer hunters to do the culling."

"We'll also need lots of volunteers to dispose of the carcasses during the day," Derek said.

Don't look at me, Corban thought. He couldn't get the stench of night terrors out of his nostrils from yesterday.

"Each mayor should plan to recruit volunteers for both tasks," Solona said.

There were reluctant nods of agreement around the table.

"Shall we meet again on fourth day to discuss a second hunt?" Solona asked.

Corban realized they were ready to adjourn and sprang to his feet. "I have a suggestion for the next hunt."

"Any ideas should be presented to the new guild master," Derek said.

"But this is something we need to work on right now." Curious and skeptical faces focused on his, but he pressed on. "We've discovered that some Strays can merge their Talents, and the results are more powerful than a single Stray's Talent. By working together, Strays might be able to protect the hunters."

"I'm already looking into it." Solona swiveled in her chair to face him. "But I doubt any combination of Talents would be an advantage against a pack of night terrors."

"Why not?" Corban asked. "You didn't see Linnea and Sergey freeze the night terror. They saved my life, and they could've saved Evans's if they'd been there."

"That was one night terror," Derek said. "There were more than two hundred in the lair."

"I appreciate your enthusiasm, Corban," Solona said, "and I'm interested to see if some Talents can be merged to aid the colony in various capacities." She paused. "But I'm not willing to put Strays in harm's way."

"Nor am I." Brooks shook her head.

Corban remembered that three of Brooks's adult children were Strays. Nehal Hong, the mayor's daughter, was his physical therapist after he was shot. "But it's all right for hunters to risk their lives?"

Solona shook her head. "That's different. Hunters are armed and experienced."

"Facing night terrors is dangerous for anyone, armed or not." Corban scanned the other faces in the room, searching for an ally. "If an experienced hunter like Guild Master Evans could be killed, no one is safe. We need a better plan and more people to help with the next hunt."

Solona fixed him with a stern look. "Merging Talents is just a theory. It'll take time to test the Strays who are willing to volunteer."

"I have the spreadsheet of the Strays' census on a datapad," Derek said. "Matching Talents should be easy."

"Finding volunteers may not be," Solona said.

"I suggest we vote on a tentative plan which includes both options." Mayor Piroux nodded to Corban.

"Thank you," he mouthed to Piroux behind Solona's back after Solona turned to face the table.

The lights in the room flickered, went off for a few seconds, and then came back on.

"Problems with the generators?" Solona directed the question to Waterfall's new mayor, Xia Papadopoulos.

"The Mechanics Guild is looking into it," was Papadopoulos's nonchalant reply. Corban sensed the mayor's concern, but her answer seemed to satisfy everyone else.

"Two nights culling them from the sentry lofts, one night to evaluate their remaining numbers, and let's say two additional weeks to test the merging Talents theory with volunteer Strays," Derek said. "Does that sound reasonable?"

Corban nodded, although he thought several mayors weren't optimistic about including Strays in the next hunt.

"All in favor?" Solona asked.

All hands were in the air. Corban kept his hand by his side since he didn't have a vote.

"Then we'll meet in two weeks and reevaluate the plan for the second hunt. Derek, please look at the census and summon Strays to Brida's infirmary for me, starting tomorrow morning. Maybe two at a time, every half hour?"

"It'll take a long time." Derek frowned. "More than two weeks."

"Just call on the ones with Talents that could be used for hunting." Solona got to her feet.

"What about the Strays in Lakeside?" Mayor Brooks

turned to Derek. "Were they interviewed for this census?"

Derek's shoulders slumped. "Darkness, I forgot. We surveyed the Strays in Brida, right after the internment."

"I think you'll want to include everyone in this merging experiment." Brooks rose from her chair. "If you're looking for specific Talents to test, you'll need their information."

"I'll do it." Corban couldn't believe the words coming out of his mouth, but he appealed to Solona's astonished expression. "Nikki and Jing can run the apothecary without me for a few days. I'll set up a table outside the dining hall and interview Strays."

"I'll let you use my datapad." Brooks offered him a cautious smile.

"Thank you, ma'am." Corban nodded.

"I'll need the information as soon as possible," Derek said. "You're sure you won't need help?"

"I can manage." *Am I crazy,* Corban thought, *or delirious from lack of sleep?*

"Ride back to Lakeside with me, and we'll get you set up," Brooks said.

"Yes, ma'am."

***

"Here, I made a sign for your table." Jing unrolled a banner of sorts. It consisted of four sheets of paper taped end to end with *Strays please report here* written in charcoal, one word per page.

"It doesn't say why." Corban covered a yawn. It was close to lunchtime, but he knew he'd be working until long past the dinner hour.

"There wasn't enough room." Jing secured one corner to the front of the table with a small rock, then did the same with the other corner. She weighed down the sagging middle with a third rock.

"Thanks." Corban set up a folding chair and opened a new file on Mayor Brooks's borrowed datapad. "What should I ask each Stray?"

"Name, guild, Talent, and where they live should be enough."

Corban sensed her disapproval. "Something on your mind?"

Jing folded her arms and regarded him with a frown. "You don't have to be involved, you know. You and Thane aren't hunters anymore."

"I know." Corban settled in the chair. "But this was too important to wait around for someone else to volunteer."

"I don't see how involving more people in hunting night terrors is a good thing," Jing said.

Corban felt a nudge of impatience. "I think yesterday's disaster proves the Hunters Guild can't do it alone."

"You told me the sentries are planning to shoot night terrors from the walls tonight and tomorrow night. You don't think it'll be enough to cull the packs?"

"I'm sure it'll help, but Derek thinks we need to destroy the dens." Corban focused on the screen and began creating a spreadsheet. He opened his mouth to ask her about Nikki but caught himself. *No, Nikki will talk to me when she's ready.*

"I need to get back to the apothecary." Jing turned away. "Good luck."

Corban wanted to call after her with something witty or reassuring, but his mind went blank. He watched her walk across the cobblestone street toward the marketplace but was brought back to reality by a familiar voice.

"What's all this?"

Corban turned in his chair to face three people about to go inside the dining hall. He forced a smile as he recognized Nehal Hong. The two dark-skinned men on either side of her were probably her brothers. "I'm taking a census of the Strays in Lakeside."

"Why?" Nehal squinted at him.

"We need to know everyone's Talents," Corban said, "so we can organize."

"Isn't it too late?" The man in a gray Tanners Guild apron furrowed his brow. "If we were organized, your uncle wouldn't have exiled most of the Strays."

"Ranveer"—Nehal jabbed him in the gut with an elbow—"be nice." To Corban she said, "You'll have to excuse my immature brother. He doesn't have a filter for his big mouth."

"It's a valid question." The other man, in jeans and a colorful plaid shirt, spoke up. "Why do they want our information now, and who's asking for it?"

Corban didn't like being put on the defensive, but he realized this question would be voiced by every Stray he interviewed. He tamped down his impatience. "Solona Zegarelli and Brida's mayor, Derek Graham, are trying to figure out how to best utilize our Talents to benefit the colony."

"But—" Plaid Shirt began.

"Just answer his questions, Kabir." Nehal aimed an elbow at Kabir's midsection, but he dodged it. "This is important. It might save lives."

Corban nodded, grateful to have her support. "This will only take a minute." He typed *Nehal Hong* under the *names* column. "I already know your Talent is touch, and you're in the Medics Guild. I just need to know where you live."

"Next door to the infirmary," she said. "Apartment N2."

Corban finished filling in her information before looking into the skeptical face of the man she'd called Ranveer. "Name?"

Eight more people approached the table while Corban was entering the information for Nehal's brothers—Ranveer Brooks, who was telepathic, and Kabir Brooks, who was telekinetic. Corban put an asterisk by Kabir's name as he thanked them and greeted the next person in line.

"Are you a Stray? Tell me your name?"

Four hours later, Corban was grateful he didn't have a desk job. He took a minute to stand and stretch but was forced to return to interviewing Strays as the early dinner crowd congregated outside the dining hall. By evening, he'd recorded the information for ninety-eight Strays and knew there was at least one hundred more living in Lakeside. Since most apartments had kitchens, few colonists ate all three meals in the dining halls. He'd have to be patient and hope for a new turnout of Strays at breakfast. A few Survivors frowned at him as they passed, but Strays, for the most part, were willing to talk.

"Do I have to give you my address?" one young woman had asked.

"How else would we be able to contact you?" Corban suppressed a weary sigh.

"Survivors like your uncle could use addresses to track us down."

"I promise it won't happen again." Corban returned her scowl. "This information will be used by Stray leaders."

"How can I be sure?" she'd asked.

Corban was tempted to say trust me, but since she already knew he was Leighton Abrams's nephew, he suspected it would be a stretch to earn her trust. "Fine, I don't need your address. Name?" He'd asked the next person in line.

"Having fun?" Thane brought him a plate of food, empty cup, and pitcher of water before heading inside to eat with Jing.

"Thanks." Corban ignored the question and the cup, and chugged half the pitcher.

"Want to help me snipe night terrors from the roof tonight?" Thane asked.

Corban choked on a mouthful of water. "I thought the sentries were in charge."

"How many sentries can handle a firearm except the ones at Brida?"

"Good point." Corban bit into a drumstick before replying. "I guess it means I should help too."

"You might want to get some sleep and come to the gates for the after-midnight shift." Thane turned away. "See you later."

Nikki's going to be furious I volunteered for another task. Corban finished the drumstick before greeting another curious face in front of his table. "Name?"

ELEVEN
DOUBTS

At dinner, Thane didn't mention to Jing that he'd volunteered for night hunting. His conscience nagged him to be honest with her, but he'd grown weary of the arguments. After spending most of his life as an overprotective older brother, it felt strange to be under the watchful eye of an overprotective fiancée. He reminded himself she was right to be concerned about his safety when it came to hunting night terrors, so she wasn't trying to control him.

At least he hoped Jing wasn't trying to control him. He was aware of her perfectionist tendencies, but they'd seen each other at their worst, physically and emotionally, and were still together. Despite her emotional volatility, Jing stayed calm in an emergency. *She has her priorities straight, right? She's mature enough to get married, right?*

I'm not having second thoughts, am I?

Thane forced the doubts to the back of his mind and kept to safe topics of conversation during the meal, such as, "How's the fish?"

"Dry." Jing covered her celadon trout with tartar sauce. "How was work today?"

"Good." When she stopped chewing and peered up into his face with those almond-shaped brown eyes that made his insides spin, he elaborated. "I like working with Bertram. He's a good supervisor. We made one hundred arrowheads today."

Oops. He forced his face into a mask, but Jing latched onto the slip.

"Why were you making arrowheads?"

"It's my job, *meili*. We have to help the hunters restock their quivers for the next hunt." Thane added more reassurance. "The hunt I *won't* be participating in except to listen from a safe distance." He reached beneath the table and gave her knee a gentle squeeze.

Jing appeared mollified, until Nikki slid into a chair at their table with a half-empty plate and stony expression. "You have to talk to him," Jing told her.

"Talk to who?" Thane asked. "Corban?" When the women exchanged a frown, he persisted. "Talk to him about what?"

"It's nothing," Nikki said in a tone Thane took to mean it was something important. "I just need more time."

"More time for what? Did I miss something?" Thane scooped a forkful of mashed potatoes.

"You and me both." Jing finished her last bite of trout. "You didn't say anything to Corban when you walked by his table? He's been out there all day."

"I know." Nikki studied her plate of salad and purple crawler filet but made no attempt to pick up her fork. "Good for him for volunteering. I'm sure Mom was pleased."

As much as Thane loathed relationship drama, he felt it was his duty to say something in case Corban needed defending. "Anything you want to share?"

"No." Nikki kept her eyes on her plate.

"I'm sure whatever happened was just a misunder-standing." Jing used her wheedling tone, but Nikki didn't react. "You two can work it out."

"Like I said, I need time. Excuse me." Nikki pushed back from the table and escaped with her untouched plate.

Thane and Jing exchanged a perplexed frown. He focused his Talent, following Nikki's footsteps as she dropped her plate at the dishwasher's alcove and left the crowded dining room. She didn't say a word to Corban outside the doors.

He heard Corban interrupt the Stray he was inter-viewing to call after her, "Nikki, can we talk?" but she kept walking. "Sorry, ma'am." Corban sounded upset as he turned back to the interviewee. "Tell me your Talent again."

Thane dragged his attention back to Jing, who was saying, "I have no idea what's going on with them." She pushed her plate away.

"I can guess," Thane said. "Corban had a premoni-tion."

Jing frowned. "Don't tell me—he saw her try to cut off his head again?"

"He usually tells me about his dreams, but he hasn't mentioned one in a long time." He almost slipped and said, "Since the one about the *Unity* explosion," but didn't want to remind Jing of her father, who'd per-ished in the blast.

"Whatever it was, it's obviously upset her." Jing fin-ished her water. "It must be serious because Nikki can't go more than a few hours without touching him. It's like they're magnets drawn to each other."

"I was going to say the same thing," Thane said. "Corban told me they share a light."

Jing nodded. "I can't tell if whatever they share is mental, emotional, spiritual—"

"Or maybe all three?"

"All I know is that Nikki glows whenever she's with Corban."

"Glowing is how I'd describe it too." Thane nodded, urging Jing to continue.

"I've known Nikki all my life, and I've never seen her this happy except when she's with him."

"Corban said it was like sharing the same soul."

Jing snorted. "That's weird."

"Yes, it's weird to us, but it's real to them." Thane finished his apple juice. "It's a small colony. I hope they can work it out because I can't imagine either of them being happy with anyone else."

"Are you happy with me?" Jing batted her eyelashes at him.

Thane froze for a moment, afraid to say the wrong thing, and Jing's smile vanished. "Of course I am!" He realized he was overcompensating for his hesitation with forced enthusiasm and tried to dial it down. "You just surprised me with the question." He leaned over and gave her a kiss, aware that dozens of people were watching with disapproval from the other tables. "I wouldn't have asked you to marry me if you didn't make me happy," he whispered in her ear.

Jing appeared satisfied with the answer. Maybe too satisfied, as she displayed her dimples and said, "Good, let's talk about the wedding. So, I was thinking I want to use peonies in all the decorating and on the cake. You like peonies, don't you?"

Thane suppressed a sigh with effort.

***

When he'd managed to say goodnight to Jing, after spending ten minutes gently prying himself free of her embrace outside the door to 26S, Thane hurried to the apartment he shared with Corban on the third floor of the west wall.

Corban was sitting at the kitchen table, loading his spare magazine. His face and forearms were bright pink. Thane noted a jar labeled *aloe vera* next to the box of cartridges. "Long day?"

His brother grunted. "I'll set an alarm for midnight, but don't be surprised if I sleep through it."

Thane took a seat at the table and picked up Corban's pistol. He racked it to test the slide and wiped down the grip and barrel with the hem of his T-shirt. "How many Strays did you interview today?"

"Gun oil stains, you know. Use the rag next to the sink," Corban said. "One hundred and sixteen. I'll need to catch the breakfast crowd early to interview the rest."

"Maybe you should skip the hunt tonight. I'm sure there'll be at least half a dozen people with guns."

"But you don't know," Corban said.

Sometimes Thane resented his brother's ability to perceive the tiniest fib. "I have no idea, but I'm sure I can take care of the whole pack by myself, if necessary."

"I've had my fill of culling the disgusting beasts." Corban set down the full magazine and sighed.

"Something on your mind?" When Corban didn't reply, Thane added, "Trouble with Nikki?"

Corban pursed his lips. "Sometimes I really hate my Talent."

Thane opted to skip the sympathetic response and got straight to the point. "Premonition?"

Corban hesitated before nodding.

"Want to tell me about it?"

"No." Corban uncapped the jar of aloe vera and dipped two fingers into the clear gel. "And I shouldn't have told Nikki either." He rubbed some aloe on his forearms.

Thane waited to see if he would offer more, but Corban focused on coating his burned skin with the gel. "Whatever it is, I hope she gets over it," Thane said.

Corban snorted. "She's mad because she feels like she doesn't have a choice anymore, because I told her about our future."

Although his curiosity was piqued, Thane kept his mouth shut. He set an elbow on the table and rested his chin in his hand, sending the message that he was willing to wait as long as it took.

Corban frowned at him for a minute before sighing again. "I saw us with a baby. Our baby."

Thane's chin slipped off his hand, and his face hit the table with a dull thud. "Darkness!" He brought his head up, rubbing his forehead. "What possessed you to tell her that?"

"I don't know! And I didn't tell her. I let her see my memory. I knew she wouldn't like it, but I was afraid she'd discover it eventually. You don't know what it's like having your whole mind open to another person. Trying to hide it from her was stressful."

Thane grimaced. "And now she feels pressured, and she resents you for it. Completely understandable."

"I've ruined everything." Corban bit his lip. "She hates me now."

"She doesn't hate you. If you saw yourselves to-gether"—Thane gulped—"with a baby, in the future, you know she's going to come around in time. Nothing either of you do will change what you saw."

"Nikki knows," Corban said, "which is why she's mad."

"All you can do is be patient and give her time to accept it."

Corban's shoulders slumped. "That's what she said too." He dabbed some aloe onto his cheeks and nose. "I think I will skip the hunt tonight. I'm exhausted."

Thane nodded, got to his feet, and picked up Corban's pistol and spare magazine. "I'll need as much firepower as I can carry."

"I feel sorry for the volunteers who have to clean up the mess in the morning." Corban pushed himself up and walked across their small sitting room to the bedroom. "Good luck and goodnight."

"'Night."

***

Unlike his brother, Thane appreciated his own Talent. It was useful and never got him in trouble unless he eavesdropped on an awkward conversation. He recalled a few of those, like the time he'd overheard Jing confess to Nikki, "Thane is wonderful. I can't wait to get married and have babies with him."

That one scared Thane, and he'd tried to distance himself from her afterward. *Obviously I couldn't stay away for long. Darkness, that girl can kiss.*

He thought about the recent premonition as he walked to Lakeside's main gates, weighed down with Corban's pistol, a rifle, and four extra magazines—two for each firearm—in his cargo pockets. *A baby!* He suspected Jing would have the opposite reaction to this type of premonition. *She'd be thrilled to hear she and I were having a baby—and I guess that's going to happen sooner or later.*

The pressure for Strays to reproduce made Thane uneasy, but he felt a responsibility to Vesta's survival. The colonists had worked too hard and sacrificed too much to allow the population to die out. Thane wished his future children had grandparents to shower them with love. It was difficult to imagine being a father with no adult family members to guide him.

He reached the gateway arch and tried the doorknob to the sentry station. It was unlocked. The tiny sentry office was vacant, so he climbed the spiral staircase to the third-floor catwalk above the closed gates.

"About time you got here." Rupert Conquist was waiting for him at the top, a large rifle by his side.

"I thought you were taking a week off for your honeymoon." Thane gripped the railings on either side of the narrow platform and followed Rupert across the rickety grating to the center of the catwalk.

"Yasmin said this was more important. Brida has enough sentries, so she sent me here to help you."

"I'll be sure to thank her next time I see her."

Both young men eyed the snarling pack of night terrors gathered beneath the spotlight in front of the gates. The din was already deafening, but Thane was able to tune it out. He switched off the safety on his rifle. "When did you learn to shoot?"

"Yesterday." Rupert laughed. "But this is like fish in a barrel—isn't that the Earth expression? There's so many it'll be hard to miss."

"I'm sure it won't be as easy as you think." Thane raised the rifle to his shoulder and leaned over, taking aim at a white muzzle dripping with saliva. "Ready when you are."

TWELVE
MERGING

The longer Nikki avoided Corban, the more her depression grew. She wasn't able to muster the energy to do anything productive. Even eating and sleeping lost their appeal.

The sleeping problem was exacerbated by the constant crack of gunshots and the relentless howling of night terrors outside the fort, making it impossible to close her eyes. Somehow, Jing slept through the racket. Nikki wondered if Thane knew Jing snored. *I guess he'll find out soon enough,* but then she remembered, *he can switch off his hearing. How convenient.*

With daybreak came welcomed silence, but Nikki knew she'd oversleep if she stayed in bed. She got up and took a long shower to wake up. The dining hall wasn't open this early, but it made no difference because she wasn't hungry. She let Jing sleep and headed to the apothecary, with a half-hearted plan to start bottling the alfalfa in the dehydrator.

Few people were stirring. As Nikki walked down the cobblestone Main Street toward the marketplace, she assumed there'd be little risk of running into Corban. It was too late to take an alternative route when she came in sight of the dining hall.

"Nikki!" Corban catapulted from his chair at the census table and hurried across the street toward her. "Please wait!"

She slowed her steps but didn't stop. "I told you I need time. Don't you understand the concept of patience?" She made no effort to hide her exasperation.

Corban paused a meter from her, his expression downcast. "I wanted to tell you again: I'm sorry."

"It's too late for that." Nikki forced herself to stop and face him. "Although you did try to warn me that I wouldn't want to see the premonition, so it's partly my fault."

"I miss you." He reached for her hand, but she took an evasive step back. "It hurts to be separated from you. I feel like my energy's fading."

Nikki bit her lip. She felt the same way but didn't want to admit it. "I don't know if I can accept knowing my future. I know you can't help it," she added, noting the flicker of pain in his eyes. "You can't control your dreams any more than I can control which memories I see if I bump into someone."

"If it weren't for my premonitions," Corban said, "we never would've met."

She shook her head. "We would've met in the library that day."

"Yes, but I wouldn't have *recognized* you. I wouldn't have gotten to know you." He managed a brief smile but turned serious again. "You wouldn't have had any reason to save my life."

Nikki made an effort not to roll her eyes. "If you're going to say we were destined to be together—"

"I wasn't." Corban extended his hand again, his expression hopeful.

She hesitated, fists clenched at her side. "I don't know how you cope with your Talent. I can't imagine the stress you have to deal with every time you have a premonition."

"I could say the same about you. Before the moment you cut off Uncle's head and fell on me, you were afraid to touch anyone. It must've been so isolating. I can't imagine how stressful it would be to see every memory in a person's mind. My memories would shock anyone, but you were determined to see past them." He moved closer and succeeded in capturing her hand.

All of Nikki's anxiety melted away. She shut her eyes and allowed the warmth and light to fill her. It was like being lost in the wilderness, dying of thirst, and Corban showing up to offer her a cold, delicious beverage. How could she not drink when her body and mind craved relief? *I'm addicted to you,* she thought. *I can't stay away, even when I'm mad at you.*

I realized that when we're together, I don't feel any stress, Corban thought. *All I feel is—I don't know how to describe it—peaceful?*

Nikki opened her eyes and studied his burned cheekbones and nose with sympathy. *Content?*

Complete. Corban hesitated. *Even if I couldn't see my future, I know I'd want you in it. I don't want to lose you, Nikki.*

Nikki let go of her last remnant of pride and threw her arms around him. *I'm sorry I got so angry. I overreacted. It's just . . . I'm not ready to think about being a mother—*

I understand. I'm sorry my premonition made you uncomfortable. His arms around her waist were hesitant at first, but then he pulled her close, relief radiating from him like the heat from his Ilios-burned skin.

I'm sorry you thought you needed to hide it from me. I know you can't control what you see in your dreams.

I wanted you to see it because I don't want to keep any secrets from you. Corban paused. *Because I love you.*

Nikki froze, shocked to hear him express it for the first time. *You do?*

From the moment I first met you, even though I was sure you were going to murder me! There, I finally said the L word. It wasn't as scary as I thought. His mouth found hers, and he lifted her a few centimeters off her feet, kissing her passionately.

She was grateful no one else was up this early to observe them making out in the middle of the street. *Let's promise not to keep any more secrets from each other.* She paused. *So we're in love. What do we do now?*

There was no hesitation in his reply. *We get married.*

Nikki broke off the embrace and leaned back to look him in the eye. *We're only eighteen storms old!*

Corban flashed the chipped-tooth grin she couldn't resist. *I don't need to wait three or four storms to be sure you're the one I want to be with forever. Marry me, Nikolasa Ramirez.*

Nikki was at a loss for words, her heart racing. She made him wait a full minute before nodding. *Yes!*

Corban whooped aloud and kissed her again, although gentler this time, as he shocked her with a new thought. *Let's go see Mayor Brooks right now and make it official.*

Slow down! My family would be furious if we eloped. Let's do it right. How about a double ceremony with Thane and Jing?

When would that be?

Knowing Jing, soon. Nikki thought.

If we get married on the same day, it'll make housing easier. Jing can move into my apartment with Thane, and I'll move in with you.

Nikki broke off the kiss to laugh. *Leave it to you to think of the practical details.*

"What in darkness are you two doing?" Jing's disapproving voice interrupted their mental conversation. She was standing two meters away, gawking at them with her arms folded.

Nikki took a step back but kept a firm hold on Corban's hand as they turned to face Jing. "We're just celebrating our engagement."

They both laughed at Jing's shocked face.

***

"Tell me you chose a date." Nikki stepped into the compounding lab and grabbed two canning jars of chilled ginger tea from the work-table.

Jing paused from her task of filling additional jars at the stove. "We did, last night. Fourth month, fourth week, seventh day."

"That's in six weeks!" Nikki smiled. "And you think Thane will be fine with a double ceremony?"

Jing shrugged, spilling a few drops of tea onto the stovetop. "They're brothers. We're best friends. Why would he mind? I'll tell him on his lunch break—if he isn't already listening to this conversation. How many more people need nausea remedies?"

"I think this is the last of the cleanup crew." Nikki hurried back into the shop and handed the jars to two pale Survivors, their coveralls spattered with night terror blood. "Drink this. It'll help."

"Thanks." The first man twisted the lid off his jar and downed several gulps, his hands shaking.

"Once we got the backhoe to the site, the cleanup went faster." The second man seemed eager to share the grisly details. "Nastiest thing I've ever seen. The beasts started devouring their dead until those two young men finished them off. Blood and fur everywhere—and the smell! I had dry heaves all morning. We kept the gates closed until midday because no one could get past the carnage."

Thanks for the visual. Nikki grimaced.

"Let's hope purple crawlers don't dig up the carcasses, or we'll have another mess to clean up." The first man lowered his jar with a sigh. "How many night terrors do you think we buried?"

"I counted fifty-eight." The second man took a swig of his tea.

The first man shuddered. "No way in darkness am I doing cleanup detail tomorrow."

"I don't blame you." Nikki was relieved when they thanked her and left the apothecary. If they'd gone on any longer, she'd need some ginger tea for herself.

"Do we need these three jars of tea?" Jing called from the back.

"Put them in the refrigerator for now. I'm sure we'll need them for tomorrow's crew."

Grateful for a break, Nikki took advantage of the empty shop to think while she made room on the acai berry shelf for the new jars of alfalfa. *I'm getting married in six weeks! I wonder if Yasmin's dress will fit me. I'll have to ask Mayor Piroux if I can borrow it.*

Her brother-in-law's voice in her mind interrupted her pleasant thoughts. *Solona wants you and Corban to come to Brida now if he's finished with the census.*

Nikki looked over at Jing, who was wiping down the long counter, noting from her friend's thoughtful frown that Derek sent her the same message. "Can you manage the shop alone?"

"I suppose, if there's no more nauseated cleanup

crew." Jing gave the countertop a vigorous swipe. "Have fun."

Nikki removed her yellow apron, tossed Jing the keys to the shop, and walked to the door. "I don't know if I'll be back tonight since it's already late. I'll have Derek or Rupert message you."

Jing smirked. "Don't have too much fun."

"I was going to say the same thing to you!"

"Thane was up all night shooting night terrors. I'm sure he'll fall asleep at dinner." Jing pouted.

Nikki laughed and left the apothecary.

***

Nikki, Corban, and Rupert caught a ride to Fort Brida in the back of a Hunters Guild truck. Nikki was grateful the guild assigned snipers for the night so ex-sentries like Isaac and Zhao wouldn't be expected to take part in the culling.

"They should've provided hunters last night," she told Rupert, "or at least armed the regular sentries."

"The hunters have been slow to respond since they're without a guild master," Rupert said. "Thane scored most of the kills last night. He's a good shot." He leaned his red head against the window of the cab and dozed off despite the bumpy ride.

Corban cradled Mayor Brooks's datapad in one arm and slipped the other around Nikki's shoulders. *Are you sure you want to marry me? No second thoughts?*

I've never been so sure of anything in my life. And going to Brida will give us a chance to tell my mom and sister.

Us? Corban sounded nervous.

Mom already loves you like a son. Don't you remember she

told you and Thane that you're part of the family, after you rescued me from your uncle?

I remember. I thought she said it to be nice. I didn't think she was adopting us.

Even after she saved your life? Nikki turned to look him in the eye. *She knocked out my father with his own rifle after he shot you, and she kept vigil over you until you healed. She also risked her life to rescue Jing from being taken aboard the* Unity, *and I'll bet she arranged for Zhao to work in Brida's apothecary so she could look after him too. She's been a mother to all of us in one way or another.*

Corban's mind was quiet for a moment. *I wish I'd known my mother.*

We'll name our first daughter after her. Nikki was half-teasing, half-serious, but she sensed a shift in Corban's mood from somberness to gratitude.

He leaned over and kissed her. *I'm looking forward to a lifetime of happy memories with you.*

Just so we're clear—it's going to be a long time before your premonition is fulfilled. There will be no—what was your mother's name?

Cassidy.

No Cassidy Zegarelli Ramirez Abrams until we're at least twenty-one.

Yes, ma'am. Corban was laughing too hard to continue kissing her. *Poor girl will be ten storms before she can spell her full name.*

***

"So why did you need to see both of us?" Nikki stepped across the threshold of Fort Brida's infirmary and handed her mother the datapad. Corban was right behind Nikki, one finger looped through the belt loop on the back of her jeans. As he entered the office and moved to stand next to her, he slipped an arm around her waist.

Nervous about telling Mom? Nikki thought.

Very. Corban gave her a gentle squeeze. *I'm already starting to sweat. Don't mind the stench.*

Nikki smothered a grin as Solona looked up from the round kitchen table she was using as a desk. The tiny front room was set up as an office, similar to the infirmary in Lakeside. She didn't respond to Nikki's query, but opened the datapad instead.

"Good, you made a spreadsheet." She flashed Corban a smile, got up from the chair, and opened the door behind her desk. "Derek?"

"Come on in," Mayor Graham called from the room beyond.

Solona nodded to Nikki and Corban, and held the door open for them. They clasped hands and walked into the spacious hospital ward.

Nikki was surprised to see there was only one bed, and it was shoved against the wall, out of the way. Derek stood in the center of the empty room, holding a pitcher of water in one hand. Linnea Savoy and Sergey Gupta stood on either side of Derek, poised like rival athletes waiting for a referee to toss a ball in the air but with each gripping an empty cup in his or her right hand.

"You're just in time to watch." Derek grinned. "These two have been practicing for days."

Solona pulled the door shut after herself and nudged Corban to move closer.

Nikki tightened her grip on Corban's hand, and they took a few steps forward. Solona moved to stand on Corban's other side.

"Ready?" Derek grinned left at Sergey, then right at

Linnea. Both nodded, staring intently at the pitcher.

"Three, two, one, go!" Derek released the pitcher, and it froze in midair, right where his hand had been. Not a single drop spilled. "Excellent! Now, just like we practiced, to Sergey first."

The pitcher glided toward Sergey. The vessel stopped a decimeter from his waiting cup and tipped forward, filling it.

"That's it, nice and slow." Derek beamed. "Now to Linnea."

The pitcher righted itself and reversed course, gliding across the space toward Linnea. The midair process was repeated as the pitcher filled her cup.

Their eyes are open! Corban's thought distracted Nikki. *It's incredible. They've achieved a higher level of control with visual focus.*

That shouldn't be a surprise, since you and I can communicate with our eyes open. Nikki wasn't aware of it until this moment. Hearing Corban's thoughts was as easy as breathing. She no longer needed to shut her eyes to concentrate.

But it took hours of practice for you to master it. When we use our Talents separately, we close our eyes.

That's true. Nikki watched as the pitcher settled to the floor at Linnea's feet. Sergey and Linnea exhaled simultaneously, and Sergey drained his cup. Linnea backed up until she reached the wall and slid down it to sit on the floor before drinking her water. Sergey wiped sweat from his brow and sent Linnea a concerned frown.

"Perfect!" Solona clapped. "Well done!"

Nikki and Corban let go of each other long enough to clap a few times, then clasped hands again.

"Now we need to see if another telekinetic Stray can join their merger," Derek said.

"Two Strays or even more," Solona said. "The possibilities—"

"Wait a minute." Sergey rounded on Solona. "I think you've demanded enough of our time. Do you have any idea how mentally exhausting this is?" He went over to Linnea and offered her a hand. "Don't you need to experiment on Strays with different Talents?"

Linnea sent Sergey a grateful smile after he pulled her to her feet. She turned to Derek. "He's right. I'm getting a headache, and I don't want to practice anymore today." She took Sergey's hand in a more-than-friends manner, and they walked out of the ward together without waiting for a response from Derek or Solona.

Nikki's mother didn't bat an eye. "So you see merging can be used for complex tasks."

"Let's try another pair," Derek said. "We know Robin Aziz is telekinetic."

"You're not expecting her to help with the next hunt!" Nikki said.

Derek shrugged and asked Solona, "Any Strays from Lakeside?"

"I haven't looked over the list yet." Solona headed back toward the office, but Corban spoke up.

"Kabir Brooks, one of the mayor's sons, is telekinetic."

"I'll message him to meet tomorrow," Derek said. "We could work with Dagmar and Malachi al-Abdullah for the rest of the day."

Corban perked up. *Malachi's my friend from West Fort. I haven't seen him since before the internment.* To Derek, he said, "Malachi was in the Hunters Guild. I'm surprised he didn't help with the hunt."

"Malachi's been depressed since the roundup." Solona's tone turned serious. "So depressed that we thought it best not to give him a firearm."

Nikki sensed Corban's shock. "Why do you want him to practice merging if he can't help with the hunt?" she asked.

"We can accomplish more than hunting night terrors by merging Talents," Derek said.

"I thought you were going to test a pair of Strays every half hour," Corban said to Solona. "Didn't you mention it at the meeting?"

"It was an unrealistic goal." Solona shrugged. "We've worked with Sergey and Linnea for a week."

"But isn't the next hunt in two weeks?" Corban asked. "Weren't we trying to have more Strays prepared to keep the hunters safe?"

"We'll need months to work on merging," Derek said. "Maybe if the night terror numbers are low after tonight's culling, we can delay the next daytime hunt."

Solona nodded. "When we've worked with all the Strays who can potentially combine their Talents, it will benefit the colony in ways we can only imagine."

I don't like the look in her eye, Nikki thought. "Care to elaborate, Mom?"

"Here's one example: it's a matter of time before the trucks wear out," Solona said. "Less than half the fleet remains mobile. We believe several Strays, merging their Talents like Sergey and Linnea, would be able to move the trucks."

"By pushing or pulling them?" Nikki scoffed.

"They'd be moving vehicles with their minds," Derek said. "We haven't tried adding a third Stray to their practice sessions, but we think it's possible."

"It sounded like neither of them wanted to practice anymore," Nikki said.

Solona grinned. "It's because they're too interested in each other at the moment. We'll give them a few days off. One good thing that's come from the intern-ment is that Strays from different forts were able to meet. A Tanners Guild young woman from East Fort would never have met a Teachers Guild young man from Orchard Valley."

Speaking of meeting Strays from other forts—now's a good time, Nikki thought. *Tell her.*

Corban squeezed her hand. *I'm not ready.* He was searching for an excuse. *Eliana's not here.*

Relax, you don't have to announce it to the entire family. Let's lure Mom back to the office and tell her without Derek overhearing.

Corban nodded. "Solona, let's take a look at the Lakeside spreadsheet together. I'd like you to see the Strays I flagged."

"Sure." Solona nodded to Derek. "Tell Dagmar and Malachi we're ready for them."

Nikki, Corban, and Solona walked back to the of-fice, and Nikki closed the door behind them. Solona reached for the datapad on the table.

Tell her, Nikki thought.

Corban's voice went up an octave as he blurted, "Nikki and I are engaged!"

Solona turned to look at them with raised eyebrows. Nikki expected her to say something about their age, but she smiled and said, "It's about time."

***

"Tell me again why you needed to see both of us, Mom." Nikki yawned and leaned her head against Cor-ban's shoulder. He was breathing deeply, already fast asleep. They were sitting on the floor with their backs against a wall in Brida's infirmary. They'd watched

Dagmar Piroux and Malachi al-Abdullah practice for two hours under Derek and Solona's guidance.

Dagmar and Malachi, who had never met before this session, could make objects invisible. By focusing on the same object, they were able to hold each illusion longer. They practiced on larger and larger objects until they succeeded in making Derek disappear for a full minute.

"Excellent!" Solona ignored Nikki's question. "And I think that's enough practice for today."

Derek reappeared, mouth gaping in astonishment. "I couldn't even see myself. It was like being a ghost."

"I have so many ideas for this Talent I don't know where to start," Solona said. "Thank you, both, for being willing to participate in the experiment."

"I don't know what you're up to, Guild Master Zegarelli, but I don't have time to wonder about it right now. I have dinner preparations to supervise, and then I have a date with Fenton DeKalb. Unless you want to see the size of my mother's favorite cleaver, you don't want her to hear that you made me miss a date."

"No, I wouldn't." Solona grinned. "Get going. Fenton's just a few storms younger than you, so Gina should be pleased."

"You're worse than Mom! Don't count the grandchildren before the second date! Fenton's Talent is scent." Dagmar lifted an arm, sniffed her sleeve, and winced. "I'm going to need time for a shower too." She flashed Nikki a mischievous grin and hurried to the door.

A serious, reserved young man, Malachi studied the sleeping Corban and said, "It was nice to meet you, Nikki," before departing.

"Who's next?" Derek asked Solona.

"No one is next!" Nikki nudged Corban awake. "We haven't eaten all day, and you still haven't told me why we're here. Corban could've delivered the datapad without me."

Derek and Solona exchanged a mysterious look. "What?" Nikki got up stiffly from the floor and offered Corban a hand.

He blinked sleepily at her. "I need a minute."

Nikki turned to face her mother and brother-in-law. "What's going on?"

"Since you asked," Derek said, "we wanted to try an experiment with you two."

Nikki folded her arms. "You know the extent of our Talents. We can hear each other's thoughts only when we're touching."

"Corban heard me when I sent you a message at the reception," Derek said.

"What kind of experiment?" Corban got to his feet, his expression guarded.

"We wanted to see if it works the other way around," Derek said. "If I sent a message to Corban, would Nikki be able to hear it?"

"It sounds simple enough," Nikki said. "What are you leaving out?"

Solona smirked. "What makes you think we have an ulterior motive?"

"The smug faces you keep sending each other when you think I'm not looking." Nikki extended a hand to Corban, and he moved next to her to take it. *They're up to something.*

You don't trust your own mother? Corban thought.

Hmm, was her response. "All right, go ahead and send Corban a message."

Derek shut his eyes.

Nikki heard, *Solona's been seeing Bertram Conquist.* It was like hearing an echo, as Corban described.

"Wait, what?" Nikki gaped at her mother. "When do you have time to date?"

Derek and Solona laughed. "So you heard me," Derek said. "Good."

"Did you make that up?" Nikki rounded on Derek.

"No, it's true," Solona said. "Bert and I have dated since the internment. It's not easy finding time to meet since we live in separate forts, but it helps to have a message service." She winked at Derek.

Nikki sputtered as Corban joined in the laughter.

THIRTEEN
SOLONA'S ADVICE

No one mentioned night terrors for two blissful weeks. Corban focused on his work at the apothecary, studied for the assistant-level herbalists' exam, and offered his opinion on the upcoming nuptials when asked, which was rare. He preferred to let the women fret over the details, as did Thane, but his brother didn't have the luxury of remaining neutral. Jing sought his opinion every minute they were together.

"Thane, should Zhao walk me down the aisle? But then who would walk Nikki? Or should Nikki and I walk together?"

"Thane, do you prefer lemon or almond for the cake? White frosting with real peonies or pink frosting flowers? Does Dagmar know how to make frosting flowers?"

"Thane, which music should we use for the ceremony? Do you think the Artists Guild has a harp player?"

"Thane, should we write our own vows or have Pastor Martin read the traditional wedding ceremony?"

"Thane, should I wear my hair up or down?"

The list of decisions seemed endless, and poor Thane had no idea how to answer any of Jing's questions. "Whatever you want is fine with me, *meili*," became his standard response, but this didn't satisfy her.

"I want your opinion," became Jing's standard response, and she'd repeat the choices, pressuring Thane to make a decision. It became a constant source of friction between them. Thane made a valiant effort to be patient, but Corban expected him to lose his temper any day now.

Corban dreaded attending the mayors' meeting to evaluate the night terror situation and decided to skip it, but Derek sent him a message the evening before: *We value your input and would like you to attend the mayors' meeting tomorrow, hour after dawn, Waterfall community council room. Thanks.*

Corban sighed. *I'll go, but no more volunteering for tasks I don't want to do. It's a big colony. Let others participate in the planning meetings. Doesn't the Hunters Guild have a new leader by now? I shouldn't have to be there representing the hunters.*

These thoughts occupied his mind as he went to bed. He wasn't looking forward to getting up extra early to ride Rupert's old bike to Waterfall.

***

The darkness was illuminated by a jagged fork of lightning, allowing Corban a split-second to see his destination. He winced as a deafening boom of thunder came right after the lightning, but he wasn't concerned for his own safety as he left the shelter of the south wall stairwell and sprinted across the open courtyard of Fort Brida. He ran blindly through the driving rain, dodging obstacles such as fire pits and picnic tables. The wind pushed back at him, plastering his clothes to his body, and the torrential rain felt like needles against his skin.

Another flash of lightning offered him a glimpse of his goal: the stairs to the upper floors of the north wall. Corban fought the elements a few more meters before wrenching open the door and stumbling into the dark stairwell. He didn't pause to appreciate being out of the punishing wind and rain as he took the stone steps three at a time. Soaked to the skin, he shivered from both cold and fear as he burst through the door into the dimly lit third-floor hallway.

"Nikki!" He heard the terror in his own voice. "*Nikki!*"

He strained his ears, desperate to hear a reply, but the thunder, howling winds, and hammering rain on the rooftop drowned out all other noises. He reached to his left until he located the wall and used it as a guide to navigate the hallway. "*Nikki!*"

***

"Corban!" There were firm hands on his shoulders, shaking him. "Wake up!"

"Stop." Corban blinked up at Thane, who released him and straightened up.

"You were shouting, 'Nikki,' in your sleep."

It took Corban a minute to get his emotions under control. "It was just a nightmare."

"Nice try, but I'm betting it was a premonition."

Corban blinked at the dim light coming through their bedroom window and guessed it was almost dawn. "I don't understand what was happening."

Thane sighed and backed up to sit on his own bed.

"There's always missing details. Why were you shouting her name?"

Corban took some deep breaths, trying to slow his racing pulse. "I was out in the storm, in Fort Brida, searching for her. I ran to the third floor of the north wall, but I don't know why I thought she was there. All I know is I was desperate to find her."

Thane scratched his unshaven chin. "That's the first time you've had a specific time frame for a premonition."

Corban sat up and shivered as the air touched his sweat-soaked torso. "I ran across the courtyard, from the south wall to the north wall, and climbed to the third floor, screaming for her. That's all I saw before you woke me."

"Darkness." Thane stood and went to the window, which faced the interior of Lakeside. "Is this going to happen during the next storm or the storm after that? How do we know which storm?" He rested his palms on the sill and pressed his nose to the glass.

"We don't," Corban said.

"Sorry I woke you too early. Hopefully, you'll see more in your next dream."

Corban was amazed at his brother's blasé attitude. "What should I tell Nikki?"

Thane shrugged. "Just tell her what you told me."

"I need time to think. Please don't say anything to Jing or Nikki, at least not until after the wedding."

Thane snorted. "Fine, but good luck keeping this memory from Nikki. Remember how she reacted the last time you kept a premonition from her?"

Corban didn't reply. He got up and headed to the bathroom to shower, his mind in a whirl. *I should tell Nikki. We agreed not to keep any more secrets from each other, but isn't it better if only one of us lives with the anxiety?* He didn't know what to do.

***

Corban sat in the same seat behind Solona's chair at the mayors' meeting. He was winded from the bike ride, pedaling fast to arrive on time, although he couldn't think of a valid reason to be there.

The Hunters Guild was represented by newly elected guild master, Amir Bjoeren. Corban recognized him from the tragic daytime hunt and thought he'd spotted him in a crowd at Fort Brida. He didn't know anything about Bjoeren, personally. If Bjoeren had lived in Orchard Valley or Greenfield before the internment, they wouldn't have met, even while they were members of the same guild. Corban was impressed a Stray was appointed guild master and hoped it was a sign that Survivors were softening their attitudes toward those with Talents.

Solona called the meeting to order and said, "Guild Master Bjoeren, welcome."

Bjoeren inclined his head toward Solona without smiling.

Solona turned to Sentries Guild master Yarborough and got straight to the point. "What are the numbers, Athena?"

"With the exception of Lakeside, each fort reported between five and eight night terrors outside the gates," Yarborough said. "Lakeside's numbers are higher, around twenty to twenty-five."

"Lower than before the cullings," Mayor Brooks said, "but still worrisome. Why just Lakeside?"

"There's probably a lair near the fort," Bjoeren said.

"The numbers have remained consistent for the past two weeks," Yarborough said.

Orchard Valley's mayor, Faith Ann Jesperson, leaned back in her chair with a sigh of relief. "The numbers haven't been this low since I was a child."

"Well done, sentries and hunters," Mayor Gina Piroux said. "Corban's idea worked."

"Now we don't need to rush to organize another hunt," Derek said.

"True," Bjoeren said. "We'll keep an eye on the numbers around Lakeside and, if they increase, plan a daytime hunt at a later date."

"Much later," Brooks said.

Heads nodded around the table.

"What's the total number culled?" Solona asked.

Yarborough studied her datapad. "With all seven forts reporting, four hundred and twenty the first night, two hundred and six the second night, and if we include the two hundred and nine from the day hunt, the total culled is eight hundred and thirty-five. I think it's safe to say the packs are no longer a threat to our safety."

There was a smattering of applause at the table.

"Why are we sitting around here?" Derek asked. "Let's plan to meet next month. I've got work to do." He got to his feet. "Meeting adjourned?"

"'Bye!" Mayor Piroux was already on her way out.

"Corban?" Solona gripped his bicep before he reached the door. "I'd like a word."

He nodded. *I guess I can't escape the awkward conversation any longer.* He and Solona stood to one side of the doorway and waited for the other mayors and guild masters Yarborough and Bjoeren to depart.

Derek was the last to leave. He grinned at Corban before pulling the door shut. *Time to be interrogated, future brother-in-law? Good luck!* There was laughter in his tone. Corban didn't find the message helpful for his growing sense of trepidation.

"Have a seat." Solona resumed her chair at the head of the conference table.

Corban settled in the chair at her left. He tried to get a sense of what was coming, but it was difficult to decipher Solona's mood. "Is something wrong?"

She smiled. "Not at all. I just wanted to talk to you without Nikki present."

He shifted in his seat, waiting.

"First, I haven't had a chance to congratulate you. I'm happy you and Nikki decided to marry. I'm delighted to be gaining another son-in-law. I know you're both young, but since you have a unique extrasensory relationship, I think communication will never be a problem in your marriage. You already seem to bring out the best in each other."

Corban wondered where this was leading. He said, "Thank you," and tried not to fidget.

"Your brother's a good man, and I think of him as family too. Thane's focused, courageous, and mature. He'll have his hands full with Jing, but I think he's already proven he can weather any of her drama."

This was turning into a speech. Corban bobbed his chin once to appear attentive, but then she surprised him by switching topics.

"I want you to know I respect your Talents. Your premonitions have saved many lives." She gave him a searching look. "I know you were afraid to share your premonition about the *Unity* because of the prejudiced attitude toward Strays, but I hope you won't hesitate to speak up next time."

"Next time?" He thought of last night's premonition. *It's too early to share it with anyone, not until I know more details.*

"I didn't want to say this in front of Nikki, but when

Derek and I were testing your combined Talents two weeks ago, I thought about how your clairvoyance affects her. You've had several premonitions about Nikki. The one about the sword didn't go over well when you told her, did it?"

"No, ma'am." Her eyes narrowed, and he amended it to, "No, Solona."

She smiled. "You can call me Mom, if you like."

Corban gulped. He nodded, unable to articulate a response.

"It must be difficult seeing glimpses of the future but not being able to share them with the people you love. Nikki doesn't like knowing her future, does she?"

He shook his head. "I don't blame her. I don't like knowing my own future." He was worried Solona was about to ask about the baby premonition, but once again, she surprised him.

"What I'm trying to say is that even if Nikki is reluctant to know about her future, I want to know about Vesta's future. I need you to share your premonitions with me, especially if they show something that will affect the entire colony. Do you understand?"

"Yes . . . Mom." It felt strange saying it, but Solona beamed at him. "Did Nikki tell you—?" He started to ask but stopped himself.

"Did Nikki tell me what?" Solona tilted her head to give him a quizzical grin.

"Nothing. My last premonition was about her, and she didn't appreciate hearing it. She didn't speak to me for a few days."

Solona nodded. "You see my point."

Corban debated telling her about last night's dream, but decided it didn't fit into the "affect the entire colony" category. *I have time to figure it out. It's five months until the storm.*

Although there were no large bodies of water nearby, Vesta's annual storm was similar to an Earth hurricane or typhoon, forcing everyone to take shelter for three days while monsoon rains and one-hundred-kilometer-an-hour winds battered the colony.

"If I have a premonition about the colony, I'll tell you right away," Corban said.

"Thank you." Solona stood and waited for him to rise before giving him a hug. She was shorter than Nikki but had the same citrus-scented hair. She released him and said, "I have to get back to work."

"Apothecary?"

"Merging Talents experiments," Solona said. "I haven't visited an apothecary in weeks, although I hear Lakeside has a growing list of patients who need to see me. I shouldn't put off my medical duties any longer."

"Maybe you should recruit some help with the experiments," Corban said.

Solona laughed. "Are you volunteering?"

"No!" It came out louder than he intended, causing her to laugh harder.

"Tell Nikki to come see me soon." Solona turned toward the door. "I'd like to know what I'm supposed to wear and what time to show up for the wedding."

"You and me both." Corban waited until she was halfway down the hall before leaving the council room. He'd had enough awkward mother-in-law discussions for one day.

FOURTEEN
DANGEROUS ERRAND

"We're out of Pryorium flowers." Nikki set an empty jar on the long counter.

Corban leaned over the counter opposite her and squinted at the label. "What's Pryorium?"

Nikki returned the squint, although hers was directed at his face. "You need to know what it is, since it's going to be on the assistant-level test next week."

He ventured a guess. "Native to Vesta?"

She nodded and reached into a cabinet beneath the counter for a sheaf of papers bound together with a loop of wire in one corner. She set it on the countertop and thumbed through the pages to reach the *P*'s.

Corban recognized the guide to Vesta's herbs Nikki printed from the library ship's datafiles several months ago, but he couldn't recall anything about Pryorium.

"Here it is." Nikki smoothed out the correct page, turned the guide around, and pushed it across the counter.

Corban studied the paper. The photo of the spiky Pryorium plant was black and white because there was no color ink left in the library's printer. Pryorium had small, spherical, feathery-looking flowers, one at the end of each tall stalk, and he recognized Nikki's handwriting where *light pink* was penciled in, along with a line drawn to one of the blossoms. "What does it do?"

"It kills bacteria better than anything we've cultivated from Earth." Nikki tapped the text beneath the photo. "I'll let you read it."

"I need to read the whole guide." He frowned. "I thought I was ready to take the exam, but I guess not."

"No time for reading today. I almost forgot that Pryorium only blooms for one week during third month. I didn't think of it until I saw the empty jar." She batted her eyelashes at him.

Corban suppressed a sigh with effort. "What do you need me to do?"

"Harvest Pryorium flowers, as many as you can. The other forts will need them too."

"Where does it grow?"

"On the north shore of Gray Lake, in the marshy areas." Nikki stooped behind the counter again and rummaged in the cabinet. She stood and handed him a rolled bundle of fabric bags. "You'll need boots and gloves—the plants are prickly."

"Shouldn't you go with me?" Corban asked. "I don't know what Pryorium looks like."

"I can't. Mom finally agreed to see several patients here today, and she needs Jing and me to assist."

"What patients?" Corban was confused. Solona hadn't visited Lakeside's apothecary in weeks. As far as he knew, his future mother-in-law had moved her medical practice to Fort Brida.

"Several, um, young women," Nikki stammered, "who need her to examine their . . . you know . . . lady parts."

Corban burst into laughter. "Lady parts?"

"Well, I didn't want to embarrass you." Nikki's face turned pink.

"It looks like you're the one who's embarrassed," Corban said.

They had a good laugh, but it was cut short when Jing strolled out of the compounding lab and asked Corban, "Why haven't you left yet? We need Pryorium."

He rolled his eyes. "Since I don't even know what it looks like, I wasn't in a hurry to go slogging through the marsh by myself."

"He needs someone to go with him," Nikki said.

"It makes sense for one of you to go with me," Corban said, "since you're both familiar with it."

"*Baba* always did the harvesting." Jing shrugged. "I've never set eyes on the actual plants."

"Me neither," Nikki said.

"So what makes you think I can find it?" Corban asked. "You're hoping I get lucky and stumble onto a patch of Pryorium?"

"I don't know what to tell you," Jing said. "The flowers will bloom for a few more days, then we'll have to wait until next storm."

Nikki shook her head. "We can't wait. We need them today."

"Good morning." Solona chose the perfect moment to step inside the apothecary, with Yasmin Conquist right behind her.

"Problem solved!" Nikki said.

"What problem?" Solona set her medical backpack on the floor and put her hands on her hips. "What are you talking about?"

"We need someone to go with Corban to harvest Pryorium." Nikki grinned at Yasmin. "Someone who can identify it."

Solona turned to her apprentice midwife with raised

eyebrows.

"I don't know what Pryorium is," Yasmin said. "I came to assist Solona."

"Nikki and I can do it," Jing said. "That way one of us can wait on any customers. We'll take turns helping her with the exams."

"You don't need to know what Pryorium looks like." Nikki picked up the empty jar and held it out to Yasmin. "As long as you can taste it."

Corban scanned the women's faces, waiting for someone to explain what in darkness Nikki was talking about.

Yasmin hesitated a moment, then walked over to the counter. She took the jar from Nikki, unscrewed the lid, lowered her face to the mouth of the jar, and stuck out her tongue.

Corban was confused.

"It should be easy to locate." Yasmin set the jar back on the counter. "It's bitter and pungent, different from anything I've ever tasted."

"Good, it's settled." Nikki grinned at Corban. "And she even wore hiking boots today. You should change into yours and get going."

"My truck's parked near the gate," Solona told him. "There's no roads around the north side of the lake, but you can drive until it gets too muddy to continue. You'll have to hike the rest of the way."

"Sounds fun." Corban made an effort not to roll his eyes.

"I'll find some gloves for both of you." Jing hurried back to the compounding lab.

Corban exchanged a helpless shrug with Yasmin, who appeared bemused at this unexpected assignment. "I guess I'll get my boots," he said. "Meet you at the truck."

***

Yasmin pointed to the items on the seat between them when Corban climbed into the passenger's side of the Herbalists Guild truck. "Canteens, sandwiches, gloves, pruning shears, fabric bags—"

"Machete"—Corban added his own supplies to the pile—"and pistol."

Yasmin pressed the ignition button. "What for?"

"Just being cautious." Corban didn't elaborate, and she didn't ask. He tucked the pistol into the waistband of his jeans. He had an uneasy feeling about this errand yet didn't think the foreboding was serious enough to cancel. The gun made him feel safer.

They sat in silence as Yasmin turned left outside the gates and drove north across a stretch of open fields bordering the western bank of Gray Lake. They made slow progress, but Corban thought the off-road conditions weren't any worse than the washed-out gravel trails connecting the seven forts.

Although Corban had lived with Rupert for a few months, he knew little about Yasmin. He searched his mind for a safe topic of conversation but came up blank.

Yasmin didn't seem to mind the quiet because she didn't say anything either. When they reached a natural barrier of scrubby bushes, she parked and cut the engine.

Corban climbed from the cab and tucked the machete under his belt. He put the canteens, sandwiches, and tools into one of the fabric bags and slipped the long handles over his shoulder. "Ready?"

Yasmin tucked the rest of the bags beneath one arm. "I'll lead."

"Fine with me."

She skirted the shoulder-high shrubs until she

reached a level stretch of embankment, which was a meter higher than the shoreline. Corban followed, and they soon lost sight of the truck. Gray Lake was to their right, and Vesta's craggy mountain range began several kilometers to their left.

Corban had never set foot in this part of the colony before. He stayed close to Yasmin, taking care where he placed his feet on the damp and rocky ground.

After a kilometer, his bluedeer-skin boots were coated in mud, but neither he nor Yasmin got stuck. The marsh weeds grew higher and closer together the farther they hiked, becoming a real obstacle.

"Do you want me to lead now?" Corban drew his machete.

Yasmin grinned at him over her shoulder and shook her head. "I'll take it."

He gave her the machete, handle first, and watched in amazement as she began clearing a path for them with ease.

After two kilometers, Corban began to wonder if Pryorium was blooming this week. Maybe it was the wrong week, and he and Yasmin were wasting their time and ruining their boots traipsing through the marsh. He noted several types of vines, briars, and shrubs, but mostly they encountered mud, knee-high weeds, and an occasional purple crawler hissing from behind a rock. He heard the lake lapping the shore not far to their right, but there was no sign of any pale pink flowers.

A stiff breeze off the lake sent a ripple through the weeds. Yasmin paused, shut her eyes, and stuck out her tongue.

"How much farther, do you think?" he asked.

"I can taste Pryorium. We're close." She started

moving again, hacking her way through a wall of vines.

Corban ducked through the vine tunnel after her and found himself facing a sea of tall, prickly stalks topped with pink spherical blooms.

"I guess we found them." Yasmin smiled.

"I'd say so." Corban slipped the bag off his shoulder and removed pruning shears and a pair of gloves for her.

"You want to have lunch first?" Yasmin asked. "It looks like it'll take a long time to harvest all this."

"No, I'm not hungry." Corban grasped the nearest plant, which was tall enough to reach his shoulder, and clipped the blossom from the stalk with his shears. He tossed the Pryorium into the bag dangling from the crook of his elbow.

"Ouch! Watch your arms." Yasmin showed him a scratch on her own bare elbow. She dabbed at the spot of blood with the tip of her gardening glove. "The leaves are sharp." She started to the left, clipping blossoms and collecting them in a bag.

Corban moved to the right, wading into the vast field of Pryorium plants. It took five minutes to fill his bag, and he realized he needed another bag to continue. It took time to backtrack and locate Yasmin, who was shorter than the Pryorium.

He knew the moment he found her that something was wrong.

She was standing still, tongue out and eyes shut, her bag of blossoms and pruning shears on the ground near her feet.

"Yasmin?"

"Wait," she hissed.

Corban's sense of foreboding nudged him, hard. "What is it?"

"I taste something." Yasmin opened her eyes and

snatched up her things. "We need to leave."

"We only have two bags—" Corban began.

"We need to leave right now." Yasmin tugged on his sleeve. "Hurry."

Corban let her lead the way again. He didn't see or hear anything out of the ordinary, but it was obvious she sensed something. They moved as fast as they could over the muddy, uneven ground, in the direction of the truck.

"What is it?" he asked again. "What do you taste?"

"Shh."

Corban felt a flicker of irritation at being shushed, but he kept pace with her and didn't voice any more questions.

Yasmin stopped so fast he almost ran into her. He watched as she shut her eyes again and stuck out her tongue. "Darkness." She grabbed his wrist, keeping a firm hold on him this time. "*Run!*"

Corban ran, although he didn't know why. The thick mud tugged at his boots, making each step difficult, but he tried to increase his pace. They'd covered half a kilometer when he heard a sound that made his blood run cold.

A familiar growl echoed through the marsh.

Corban switched Yasmin's grip to his left hand and drew his pistol with his right. "Where's a tree? We need to climb one."

"There's no trees here." Yasmin kept moving, pulling him after her. "Maybe the lake? Can they swim?"

"Yes." Corban sucked in a ragged, terrified breath. "Night terrors can swim."

A pair of howls joined the first. The bloodthirsty beasts were getting closer.

"I tasted something vile when the breeze was in my

face," Yasmin said. "They must've caught the scent of my blood."

"It's all right." Corban panted. "You don't have to explain."

Yasmin's foot became entangled in a nest of vines, and she fell onto her hands and knees in the mud, spilling everything she was carrying. Corban got his left hand under her elbow and hauled her to her feet.

"Leave it," he said as she made a move to recover the machete. "There's no time." He dropped everything except his pistol. "We've got to get back to the truck."

They ran, covering only twenty more meters before the night terrors caught up to them. One of the beasts cut across their path, teeth bared and ready to pounce, while two others flanked them.

Yasmin screamed.

Corban took aim at the snarling horror two meters in front of them, hyperaware of the fact that each shot had to be precise because he didn't have a spare magazine.

He shot it between the eyes, then turned, and shot one of the night terrors behind them. The third beast hesitated, eyeing its fallen companions before crouching to lunge at them. Yasmin screamed again and grabbed Corban, throwing off his aim. The third shot missed its intended target.

Corban shoved Yasmin clear a heartbeat before the predator's heavy forepaws hit him in the chest and knocked him flat on his back in the mud. Corban found himself looking straight up the muzzle of the night terror, its jaws centimeters from his face.

He threw out his left hand and gripped the thick, furry neck, desperate to keep the sharp fangs away from his throat. He kept a grip on the pistol and squeezed the trigger. The bullet pierced the monster's abdomen. The pain startled it long enough for Corban to get his wrist into a better position.

He pulled the trigger twice, piercing its skull with the second shot. He was shocked at how much the night terror weighed as the body shuddered, collapsed, and pinned him to the ground.

"Corban!" Yasmin was hysterical. He felt her tugging at the dead night terror, trying to roll it off of him.

"Are there any more?" Corban gasped. The weight on his chest made it difficult to breathe.

"I don't know!" Yasmin sobbed. "It's not your blood?"

"I'm all right. Just please get it off me."

"I'm trying." He heard her grunt a few times as she struggled to move the body. As soon as he could free his hands enough to help her, he was able to wriggle out from underneath the grisly corpse.

Corban climbed shakily to his feet, overwhelmed with the stench of blood that drenched him from head to toe. He barely managed not to vomit. "Are there any more?"

Yasmin shook her head. "If there are, they'll smell this." She kicked at the dead night terror with her boot.

"And then we're dead, because I don't have any more bullets." Corban tucked the pistol into his waistband. "Let's get back to the truck."

His first step was wobbly, and he almost fell. Yasmin put her arm around his waist.

"Come on, lean on me. Let's get above the shoreline. The ground should be firmer."

"Good thinking." Corban was shaking from the adrenaline rush, and his mind seemed to switch off for a brief time. He allowed Yasmin to help him, barely conscious of where he placed his feet, until at last they saw the truck.

"I'll drive." Yasmin opened the passenger's side door and helped Corban inside.

"Solona's going to be mad I ruined the upholstery." Corban pulled the door shut.

"I think she'll be grateful her future son-in-law survived a night terror attack." Yasmin slipped into the driver's seat and started the engine.

"For the third or fourth time. I've lost count." He looked down at his bloodstained clothes. "I hope Nikki doesn't faint when she sees me."

"Tell her to go get her own Pryorium next time."

***

Nikki didn't faint when Corban and Yasmin walked into the apothecary, but the color drained from her face, and she placed a hand against the wall to steady herself.

Jing screamed but covered her mouth with both hands, muffling the sound.

Solona emerged from the doorway to the examination room. "What happened?" She rushed over to Corban, searching him with her eyes for injuries.

Corban waved her off. "It's all right. It's not my blood."

"Night terrors," Yasmin said. "We were fortunate only three came after us."

"I think we know where another lair is," Corban said. "The ones still stalking Lakeside live close to the Pryorium field. Sorry we didn't bring any back for you."

"I don't care about that!" Nikki ran across the shop and threw her arms around him. *I should've gone instead!*

No, if you had, you and Yasmin would've been killed. Corban didn't like to think about how close he came to dying himself. He patted the pistol at his waist. "I thought to bring this, and it saved us."

"That, and some excellent marksmanship," Yasmin said.

Solona blew out a shaky breath. "I guess I'll let Guild Master Bjoeren know he should plan another daytime hunt."

"Tell him Thane and I *won't* be participating." Corban turned toward the door. "Now if you'll excuse me, I need a shower."

FIFTEEN
THE WEDDING

Thane woke to the throes of a panic attack. "What's happening?" he shouted at the dark room.

"Whazz?" Corban muttered from the other bed. "Nightmare?"

"Worse." Thane sat up and pressed a hand over his pounding heart. He was sweaty and shaking. "Darkness, what day is it?"

"Seventh." Corban sounded more coherent but annoyed. "Although it's barely past sixth day. Go back to sleep."

"I have this overwhelming feeling that I'm about to make a huge mistake," Thane said.

Corban laughed but then turned serious. "You want to call off the wedding?"

"I . . . don't know." Thane's stomach ached.

"I think panic is a normal response to being stuck with one person for the rest of your life."

"Such a nice way to describe marriage." Thane rolled his eyes.

"If you think you can't go through with it, you'd better tell Jing now."

Thane got a throbbing pain in his forehead as he considered the social and emotional consequences of dumping the bride on her wedding day. "No, you're right. It's nerves. I'll be fine." He didn't feel fine but tried to convince himself the anxiety would pass.

"Look under the bathroom sink for something to help you sleep. There's vetiver essential oil."

"What in darkness is vetiver? You sound like an herbalist. No, there's a bottle of wine in the refrigerator." Thane climbed out of bed. "I was saving it for tonight, for the honeymoon, but I think my nerves could use it now."

Corban snorted. "You hate wine. You want to be hung over in the morning?"

"One cup to help me relax." Thane strapped on his brace and headed to the kitchen, feeling his way carefully in the dark so he didn't locate door jambs or furniture with his toes.

"Don't get drunk and start spouting poetry," Corban called after him.

"I don't know any poetry. You're thinking of Rupert." Thane found the refrigerator and squinted as the light hit his eyes when he opened the door. A ceramic jar of Orchard Valley's finest rosé, a wedding gift from his guild master, Bertram Conquist, took up the center shelf of the mostly empty appliance. He stared at it for a full minute before closing the door with a sigh.

He settled in a chair near the sitting room window and stared at the courtyard village. Thane rested his chin in his hands and studied the outline of buildings visible in the dim glow of Vesta's stars. A light went on in a window of the row house across the street but winked out after a few moments. He wondered who else was up this late. *Maybe a parent checking on their child?*

He thought about eavesdropping, but there was no point.

Is that what's bothering me? The whole fatherhood thing? As orphans raised by an abusive uncle, Thane and Corban had little experience in a traditional family setting. Thane was three storms old when their parents died from the Plague. Memories of their faces had blurred with the passage of time, but he still felt an ache inside whenever he thought of Harrison and Cassidy Abrams.

Thane and Corban had always looked out for each other, but understanding adult roles was difficult without a father-figure in their lives. *Am I scared because I'm venturing into uncharted territory?*

Come on, Thane, you've faced a night terror with nothing but a machete to defend yourself. How scary can it be to be a husband and someday a father?

Scary if you're marrying a domineering personality like Jing Kaczenski. Jing had been a tyrant when it came to planning the wedding. Thane wanted to accept her behavior as normal for any bride, yet Nikki was calm from the moment Corban proposed to her. She made no demands on Corban, and she'd reminded Jing, at least five times that Thane recalled, "Focus on the marriage, not the wedding."

It's just one day. She wants it to be special. You can smile and get through it. The mental pep talk wasn't helping, but Thane felt his adrenaline ebbing, loosening the knot in his stomach. After a few minutes, he realized how exhausted he was. *I should go back to bed.*

On impulse, he tuned his hearing to listen to the gentle sounds of Lakeside at night. Nocturnal insects buzzed, a pair of sentries discussed whether it would rain, and a mother sang a lullaby to her colicky infant. He was about to switch off his Talent when he heard a familiar voice say his name.

"I have to tell Thane. This can't wait till morning." It was Jing, and she sounded distraught.

"It's the middle of the night," Nikki's sleepy voice replied. "Go back to bed. You'll feel calmer in the morning."

Thane focused his hearing, determined to catch every word.

"I can't do it! I can't go through with it!" Jing's voice cracked. "I love him, but he's been so passive with all the planning. It's like he doesn't want to get married!"

"Darkness," Thane whispered. *She's having second thoughts too?*

"I told you not to pressure him," Nikki said. "You can be a little overbearing, you know."

"I'm not—" Jing sputtered, but Nikki spoke over her.

"Corban told me men don't care about details. They don't even care if their socks match, so expecting them to make so many decisions is overwhelming. It's your wedding—our wedding—so Thane didn't want to spoil it by expressing an opinion on every detail. He's *not* passive, but you've treated him like a slime worm these past few weeks."

"I'm"—huge sniffle—"overbearing?"

"Yes, and it wouldn't surprise me if he's wondering if he made a mistake."

Thane got to his feet and limped to the door. He paused with his hand on the doorknob, realizing he was barefoot, wearing his shabbiest pajama bottoms, and reeked of perspiration. He hurried to the dark bedroom, trying not to disturb Corban as he snatched some clothes from his dresser. He took a two minute shower, dressed, strapped on his brace, shoved his feet into shoes, and hurried to apartment 26S.

Thane paused to listen before knocking. He didn't want to disturb Nikki and Jing if they'd gone back to sleep, but all he heard was gut-wrenching sobs.

He knocked. The crying stopped, and there were footsteps, but then it got quiet as he heard Jing breathing on the other side of the door.

"It's Thane."

The door opened a crack, and Jing peered out at him. From the weak glow of the night-light in the hallway behind him, he saw that her face was blotchy-pink from crying.

Without a word, she opened the door wider, admitting him into the dark apartment. She turned on a table lamp and sank into a chair in the sitting room, gesturing for him to take the sofa.

Thane didn't sit but stood near the door with his arms folded, studying her. Her black hair looked as if she'd run through a storm, and she wore a purple stretched-out nightgown that had seen better days. She attempted to dry her eyes on one of the sleeves, without success.

"Nikki's asleep, so we should whisper." Jing's voice was thick with emotion. She sniffled and cleared her throat. "You couldn't sleep either?" She wouldn't look at him, fixing her gaze on a knot in the plank floor.

Thane didn't trust himself to speak because he knew it would sound wrong, and it did. "Maybe the wedding was a mistake."

Jing's trembling chin jerked upward, and her eyes brimmed with fresh tears. "You don't want to marry me?"

He rushed over and pulled her to her feet. "Yes, I want to marry you, but I didn't want a fancy wedding. I kept my mouth shut because I knew it was important to you, but the stress in planning it was bad for our relationship. A wedding is one day, a marriage is forever." He scooped her up in his arms. "What do you say we go wake up Mayor Brooks?"

Jing sputtered for a moment, her expression somewhere between horror and delight. "I can't go looking like this. Let me take a shower and put some clothes on."

"You look beautiful just the way you are, *meili*." Thane carried her to the door. "And you won't need any clothes tonight."

Jing surprised him by bursting into laughter. "Someone's been reading old Earth romance novels! I'll need some shoes, at least, because you're not carrying me upstairs like an overgrown baby. Give me a minute." She squirmed until he set her on her feet.

He watched in amusement as she hurried back to the bedroom, opened and closed drawers in the dark, then ducked into the bathroom, emerging five minutes later in the pink silk dress she wore when he proposed. Her hair was perfect, and there was no trace of tears on her face.

"I'm ready, Mr. Abrams."

Thane offered her his arm. "I love you, Ms. Abrams."

SIXTEEN
THE WEDDING, PART 2

Drifting in the fog of half-asleep, Nikki thought she heard voices in the apartment during the night. She assumed Jing was pacing the floor and talking to herself. *At least she stopped crying.* Nikki could have sworn she heard laughter but convinced herself she was dreaming.

When she woke at daybreak and found Jing's bed empty, she didn't give it a second thought. She took a shower and struggled to fix her hair at the bathroom mirror. She gave up trying to make it look the way Jing had styled it for Rupert and Yasmin's reception and left it long and wavy.

She went back to the bedroom to get dressed and saw Jing's wedding gown on a hanger in the wardrobe. It wasn't like Jing to wait until the last minute to get ready, but Nikki wasn't concerned. *Nervous wreck probably went for a jog this morning.*

Nikki slipped on Dagmar Piroux's borrowed wedding dress and struggled to reach the zipper in the back.

There was a knock at the door, forcing her to hold the gown closed at the back of the neck and walk to the sitting room to answer it. "Hello, Mom. Elie."

"Good morning!" Solona stepped inside. "Here, let me help you."

"It's your apartment, Mom. You don't have to knock." Nikki turned around so Solona could zip her.

"No, it's your apartment, and yes, I have to knock," Solona said. "After the wedding, it'll belong to you and Corban. I'm not going to walk in on anything I shouldn't see."

Nikki managed a wan smile. "Good point."

"You look gorgeous." Eliana gave Nikki a congratulatory peck on the cheek. She and Solona were wearing simple matching peony-pink sheath dresses, their auburn hair twisted into neat buns. "Are you wearing your hair like that?"

Nikki rolled her eyes. "Yes."

"It looks fine. I want to see Jing in her dress." Solona turned toward the bedroom.

"So do I," Nikki said. "But she's not here."

"She might be in the dining hall," Solona said. "I'm sure she'll be back soon. Derek and Zhao took Travis to get a bite to eat before we head over to the chapel."

"We're hoping a full stomach keeps him quiet during the ceremony," Eliana said.

"Who? Travis or Derek?" Nikki asked.

Eliana laughed but then said, "Mom has something for you."

"What?" Nikki's eyes flicked back and forth between them, trying to guess what they were up to.

Solona extended an open palm. "This was Grandma Zegarelli's. I want you to have it."

Nikki plucked the braided band of shiny gray metal from her mother's hand. "I thought you gave this to Elie."

"I have Grandma Ramirez's ring." Eliana showed

Nikki her left hand, where a band of golden metal adorned her third finger. "You haven't seen it because I only wear it on special occasions."

"Thank you." Solona's family wasn't sentimental about material things, so Nikki was touched to receive a family heirloom. "I promise to take good care of it."

She started to try it on, but Solona and Eliana shook their heads.

"Corban should put it on your finger." Solona took the ring back. "I'll give it to him before the ceremony."

"Speaking of ceremonies . . ." Eliana faced the front door. "Where's the other bride?"

***

Nikki sent her mother and sister ahead while she waited for Jing as long as she could.

Derek messaged her at midday. *Corban's waiting. It's past time to start. We don't know where Thane is, so everyone's getting impatient.*

I don't know where Jing is either. Nikki wished she had the ability to send a message in response. She slipped on her sandals, took her small bouquet of peonies from the refrigerator, and left for the chapel, attracting a great deal of attention in her wedding gown as she hurried down Main Street.

The Lakeside Community Chapel was a simple A-frame stone building in the center of the marketplace. It consisted of a single room with a vaulted ceiling, eight rows of pews with an aisle down the center, and a stone pulpit at the front.

As she entered the double front doors and looked down the aisle to the other side of the chapel, she saw Corban standing to the right of Pastor Martin at the pulpit. Zhao was frowning on Corban's right. Both young men were dressed in borrowed gray suits.

Fifty guests turned in the pews to gawk at Nikki before resuming their whispered conversations. She heard Travis fussing and Eliana attempting to shush him. Solona hurried over with a concerned frown.

"Where's Thane and Jing? Shouldn't we wait for them?" Nikki asked.

"Elie will have to take Travis out if we don't start now," Solona said.

"This is supposed to be a double wedding." Nikki didn't know what to do.

"Ah, there you are." Mayor Brooks stepped through the doorway behind Nikki. "I was starting to wonder if you and Corban decided to elope too."

Nikki turned to Brooks. "Thane and Jing eloped?"

Solona shook her head. "When, and why?"

"They pounded on my door in the middle of the night and asked me to marry them right then and there." Brooks spread her hands in a helpless gesture. "I woke my sons next door to be witnesses. I gave Thane the key to Lakeside's guest suite." She sent the baffled wedding guests a mischievous smirk. "I guess they slept in."

"What's going on?" Corban rushed down the aisle to join the three women. "Where's Thane?"

"Where's Jing?" Zhao called.

"They're already married." Solona raised her voice so everyone in the chapel could hear. "Thane and Jing eloped last night." There were gasps of surprise and muffled laughter as the chatter grew louder. Zhao hurried down the aisle to join the huddle.

"I don't understand." Corban's brow furrowed, but then he gave Nikki a wide-eyed once-over and smile of approval. She resisted the urge to giggle at his mixed reaction.

Zhao said, "*Mei mei* wanted a wedding. She planned all this."

"Yes, but Thane didn't. He woke up in a panic last night and told me he felt overwhelmed," Corban said.

"So he convinced her to skip the ceremony." Nikki shrugged. "If I'd known they weren't going to be here, we could've eloped too." She winked at Corban.

"Well, everyone here came to see a wedding, so let's not keep them waiting." Solona gestured for Corban and Zhao to return to their places. Mayor Brooks went to sit next to her daughter, Nehal Hong, on the third row.

Nikki took a deep breath and waited for the music to begin. She didn't know where Jing found a musician with a real harp.

"Ready?" Solona gave her a kiss on the cheek and hurried to sit on the front row next to Bertram Conquist. Rupert, Yasmin, Eliana, and Derek sat farther down the pew. Eliana bounced Travis on her knee, trying to distract him.

Jing's supposed to be next to me. It felt strange walking down the aisle alone, but Nikki stopped in front of Pastor Martin and turned to Corban with a smile. *Who cares? This is where I'm meant to be.* With no Jing to hold her flowers, she shoved the bouquet at an astonished Zhao and took Corban's hands in hers. *I love you, Mr. Abrams.*

I love you, Ms. Abrams.

Nikki barely heard anything Pastor Martin said. She gazed into Corban's eyes and waited for her cue to say, "I do." At one point, the minister paused while Corban slipped the wedding ring onto her finger, but Nikki didn't break eye contact.

This is taking too long, she thought.

Can't wait to be alone with me? Corban wiggled his eyebrows at her, and it took every gram of self-control not to laugh.

Don't turn around, Rupert's voice broke through her thoughts, *but Thane and Jing just walked in.*

Nikki wished he hadn't mentioned it because the urge to look over her shoulder was unbearable.

They're sitting on the back row, Rupert added.

Eyes on me. Corban grinned.

Eyes up here! Nikki smirked. *My mother can tell you're staring at my cleavage.*

It's all right because Bert's staring at hers!

What? Nikki started to giggle, almost missing Pastor Martin's final instruction. "You may now kiss the bride."

No tongue while everyone's watching, please, she thought.

Corban broke off the kiss to laugh.

"May I introduce Mr. and Ms. Corban Abrams," Pastor Martin said.

Nikki and Corban turned to face the chapel. Everyone was on their feet, applauding.

"Do I need to perform another ceremony?" the minister called to the back row.

"We're good, thanks!" Jing was wearing her cheongsam dress, and Thane was in his gray suit, their arms around each other's waists.

"I think we can make the reception," Thane added in a teasing tone.

***

"Couldn't we do this tomorrow?" Corban finished unloading the contents of his dresser into a *Unity* box.

"It won't take long." Nikki turned to give Rupert a

153

smile. "Thanks for your help."

Rupert rolled his eyes and bent to lift the box. "Nobody helped me and Yasmin move into our apartment."

"I did!" Zhao stuck his head in the bedroom door.

"You stood around and gave us advice on how to pack," Rupert said.

Zhao smirked. "I offered moral support."

Rupert snorted with laughter.

"I would've helped you move if I lived in Brida." Thane stepped out of the bathroom with a smaller box. "I think this is the last of Corban's stuff."

"Moving *mei mei* will take longer. She has more clothes than all of us combined." Zhao dodged a swat from his sister, fending her off with a ceramic table lamp.

"Don't drop it." Jing put her hands on her hips. "That was their mother's." She'd stayed in her pink dress, while Nikki and the men changed into jeans and T-shirts right after the ceremony.

"I know." Zhao turned serious. "It belonged to Thessa Abrams before her, and Nia Abrams before her."

"Ugh, don't start with the history of everyone who's ever touched it, *ge'-ge'*." Jing went to hold the door open for the movers.

"I have to use my Talent whenever I have an opportunity." Zhao placed the lamp in a hemp basket, which was filled with other wedding gifts, and followed Rupert out the door. "And this was woven by Fiona DeKalb, Dr. DeKalb's sister-in-law."

"Hush!" Jing shouted after him, but she was grinning.

"You know you kept that on so you wouldn't have to do any work." Nikki moved to stand beside Jing at the doorway.

"I kept it on because Thane likes it." Jing seemed

completely at ease, nothing like the uptight, micromanaging bride Nikki expected. "I'll wear my gown at the reception."

"Glad you'll be joining us since you planned every detail."

"Someone told me to focus on the marriage, not the wedding." Jing winked at her.

"I think several someones told you that, *meili*." Thane paused to give Jing a big sloppy kiss before stepping out of the apartment with two boxes in his arms.

Nikki waited until Corban, Thane, Rupert, and Zhao turned the corner to the south corridor before confronting Jing. "What possessed you to elope a few hours before the wedding?"

Jing smirked and walked to the kitchen. "It's hard to say no to a man who sweeps you off your feet in the middle of the night." She opened the refrigerator. "Ooh, want to try the wine?"

"No, thanks." Nikki took a seat at the messy kitchen table. "I'd love a drink of water though."

Jing filled two cups from the faucet and sat in the other chair.

"Don't you want to supervise them moving your things?" Nikki drained her cup.

"Already boxed up most of it yesterday, so there's nothing to supervise. Zhao knows which dresser's mine and which is yours."

"You sound so calm." Nikki stood to refill her cup. She frowned at the pile of dishes in the sink, found a dishcloth, and turned on the faucet.

"I think I'm calm because it's over." Jing got up and searched the kitchen drawers. "There has to be a towel here somewhere. How can men live like trashbirds?

This place desperately needs to be cleaned and organized." She added, "The anticipation and all the wedding plans made me a little tense."

"A little?" Nikki lathered the dishcloth with the tiny sliver of soap and started washing.

"What about you?" Jing rinsed and dried the clean plates Nikki handed her. "Are you nervous about the honeymoon?"

"The only thing I'm nervous about is getting pregnant while I'm still a teenager." Nikki gave her a sideways glance. "You?"

"I didn't give it a single thought last night." Jing giggled.

Nikki focused on scrubbing a juice pitcher. "So a baby by your next birthday?"

"Sure, why not?" Jing was thoughtful for a moment. "Do you think there's an herb that'll help me conceive a boy?"

"No." Nikki made an effort not to roll her eyes. "You have to take whatever God gives you."

"I'm sure there must be something. I'll ask Solona."

"No!" Nikki rounded on her. "Don't tell Mom you want a boy!"

Jing took a step back, her eyes wide. "Why not?"

"Because she'll get very angry, angrier than this." Nikki pointed to herself and took a deep breath to calm down. "Mom had a baby between Eliana and me, but he was stillborn. My slime worm father blamed her, and then he was disappointed when I was born because he wanted a son. When Eliana and I became Strays, it gave him the perfect excuse to reject us. Wanting a boy is a very sore topic with Mom, and I'd advise you to never mention it."

"I didn't know you had a brother," Jing whispered. "I'm sorry."

"Didn't you ever wonder why there's seven storms between Elie and me? Be grateful for any child you have, no matter which gender." Nikki turned back to the dishes. "There are colonists who're going to envy us ten storms from now. They might even hate us."

"Normals." Jing nodded.

"I wouldn't be surprised if they start asking us to be surrogates." Nikki felt a pang of disgust.

"Asking Strays, you mean," Jing said. "I'm safe."

Nikki made an effort to lighten the mood. "You and Thane can have enough babies for all of us."

Jing laughed. "Any baby of Thane's will be a giant. Solona will have to install a zipper on me because they'd all be cesarean deliveries. I'll be so huge when I'm nine months pregnant I won't be able to walk."

"You'll have to drag yourself across the floor like a purple crawler."

They were laughing and cleaning the kitchen when the young men returned, arms loaded down with boxes of Jing's possessions.

"What's so funny?" Zhao set a box on the kitchen table.

"You are, *ge'-ge'*," Jing said. "You forgot to walk me down the aisle."

Zhao started to protest, but everyone else burst into laughter. "Fine," he said, "then you'll sit on the back row for my wedding, *mei mei*."

"I'll need to sit because I'll be an old lady by then." Jing smirked.

***

The Abramses' Lakeside reception took place in the

157

marketplace park, which was a simple grassy area bordered by flowering bushes. Nikki was grateful Jing agreed to scale back the lavish party to a receiving line and wedding cake. The Artists Guild musicians weren't too disappointed to have the evening off.

She was also pleased to see Jing in her frilly wedding gown, since her friend had harangued the Tailors Guild to sew it to her exact specifications. Nikki was sure the seamstress in charge of Jing's fussy white frock was happy to see the last of her. *Ten bottles of essential oils wasn't enough payment to put up with Her Majesty.*

Corban's arm around Nikki's waist helped keep her calm. She held her bouquet in both hands to ward off anyone who didn't know about her Talent, but Corban acted as a buffer too. He would shake hands and direct the person in line to Thane on Nikki's left.

Thank you, she told him for the umpteenth time. *Aliza looked like she wanted to hug me.*

She did, but she understands. Corban and Thane both hugged their former nanny, Guild Master Yarborough's daughter, Aliza, who was delighted to meet Nikki and Jing.

"These boys deserve happiness after all the darkness their uncle put them through," Aliza said.

"I'll do my best to make him happy," Nikki said.

"Me too!" Jing laughed.

"Congratulations!" Emily Vaughn, Corban and Thane's former teacher, gave them each a kiss on the cheek as she went down the line. Nikki was grateful hers was an air kiss.

She remembered. She's such a kind lady. Ms. Vaughn saved our lives that night.

I wish I could've saved her daughter's life.

No gloomy thoughts. Nikki smiled at the next person in line. *Mayor Piroux! Remember she saved our lives too by*

158

smuggling us out of the fort?

Mayor Piroux and Dagmar rescued Thane from the back of the truck during the internment.

We're fortunate so many people were willing to help us, Nikki thought.

Despite what Uncle thought, not all Survivors hate Strays.

Please don't mention that horrible man again. Nikki jabbed Corban with an elbow.

Gina and Dagmar Piroux greeted them warmly, followed by Fenton DeKalb, who was holding Dagmar's hand. Dr. Lorna DeKalb was right behind her son. Nikki thought the carpenter appeared nervous but didn't blame him with two strong-willed mothers pressuring the newly engaged couple for grandchildren.

I guess they had a second date. Corban struggled to hold back a laugh.

"The dress looks great on you!" Dagmar turned to Fenton with a mischievous grin. "You'll be seeing this on me in a few months."

Her fiancé managed a nervous smile but didn't comment. Nikki imagined Fenton was as overwhelmed as Thane had been when Jing was in charge of wedding plans.

"My gift to you," Mayor Piroux told Corban and Nikki, "is a dozen cinnamon rolls anytime you're in West Fort."

"That's the best gift we've had all day!" Corban gave her a hug. "Thank you."

"You too." The mayor hugged Thane. "Cinnamon rolls, pastries, whatever you like."

"Can you make steamed buns?" Jing asked.

Nikki bit her lip to keep from laughing at the startled expression on Mayor Piroux's face. "What in darkness are steamed buns?"

"Never mind, *mei mei*," Zhao spoke up on Jing's other side. "I'll make steamed buns for you."

"You'll have to show me how to make them, Zhao." The mayor hugged Jing and moved down the line to Solona to the left of Zhao.

Nikki's cheeks ached from smiling. *I wish we'd eloped too.*

I gave you the opportunity, if you recall.

I didn't have time to think about it. You said, "Let's elope," two minutes after you asked me to marry you. She covered a yawn. *I'm exhausted. I've had enough celebrating for one day. I want to go home and get out of this stupid dress.*

Corban paused for a beat. *I can help you with that.*

Nikki felt her face growing warm. "Is it time to cut the cake yet?" she asked Jing.

SEVENTEEN
SHARED PREMONITION

Soaked to the skin, Corban shivered from both cold and fear as he burst through the door into the dimly lit, third-floor hallway of Brida's north wall.

"Nikki!" He heard the fear in his own voice. "Nikki!"

He strained his ears, desperate to hear a reply, but the thunder, howling winds, and hammering rain on the rooftop drowned out all other noises. He reached to his left until he located the wall and used it as a guide to make his way down the hall. *"Nikki!"*

A door beneath his hand swung open unexpectedly, and Corban fell sideways into an apartment. A pair of hands seized him under the arms and hoisted him to his feet.

"What are you doing here?" Sergey Gupta asked. "You don't even live in Brida. Why didn't you evacuate with the rest of the fort?"

"I couldn't leave without Nikki!" Corban turned to face Sergey. "Have you seen her?"

"She left a few minutes ago to look for you. Solona went with her." Linnea Savoy's gentle voice was tinged with fear. "We'd help you look, but we have to be ready."

Corban was aware of several more people in the apartment, their nervous voices muted by the storm raging outside, making it impossible for him to identify them. "Who else is here, and why did you stay behind?"

"I'm here to keep watch."

He noticed Isaac Nomura for the first time. His former roommate was sitting on the floor, a towel wrapped around his shoulders. Water dripped from the ends of Isaac's black hair as if he'd just come in from the rain too. "Obviously, it's impossible to see anything once the rain started."

It was on the tip of Corban's tongue to ask *what* they were expecting, when they all heard a noise that drowned out the storm. There was a roaring boom in the distance, outside the fort, similar to the *Unity*'s explosion.

"Get to the roof!" Sergey shouted.

Panic shot through Corban. "*Nikki!*"

***

"Corban, wake up!"

He jerked awake to discover Nikki sitting up next to him in the bed, one hand on his shoulder, shaking him. "Wake up! You're having a premonition."

His heart was pounding as he reached up to grasp her hand, wondering what she'd seen.

Your arm was around me while we were sleeping, so I saw all of it, she replied before he finished the thought. Nikki studied his face, her mouth pinched into a thin line. *I'm sensing from your guilt that you've had this premonition before.*

Corban nodded and sat up. *A few weeks before the wedding.*

Why didn't you tell me? You promised no more secrets!

His guilt turned to shame. *I didn't want to worry you.*

That's no excuse, Corban!

I was going to tell you, I swear. I needed a little more time to figure out the details.

Three months isn't a little more time!

I was hoping to have the dream again so I'd have more information to share with you. He tried to help her see reason. *Remember the baby premonition?*

How could I forget? She rolled her eyes. *What's that premonition got to do with this one?*

I knew you'd react the same way. Not knowing why I was searching for you during the storm has weighed on my mind, and I wanted to spare you the worry.

He sensed Nikki's temper thawing, but she wasn't letting him off easy. *I appreciate your concern, but you can't shelter my feelings anymore. Your premonitions affect both of us. I need to know about them, no matter how frightening they are. Seeing one while I was asleep was a shock. I would've preferred to know about this the first time you had it. I'm sure this won't be the last time we see each other's dreams.*

So we should sleep in separate beds? Corban cracked a smile, but it faded beneath her scowl.

It's not funny. She shook her head and grasped both his hands in hers. *We have to face your premonitions together. You need to share them with me right away. Agreed?*

He nodded, prodded by the weight of his guilty conscience. *I promise it won't happen again.* He leaned toward her, but she didn't seem ready to forgive him yet.

Why were you yelling for me?

I don't know. He made an effort not to pout as she avoided his kiss.

Why were we in Fort Brida? Wouldn't we take shelter here during a storm? Nikki didn't give him a chance to answer. *Why did Sergey say Brida was evacuated? And what did Linnea mean by they had to be ready? Ready for what? What was*

163

Isaac watching for, and who else was with them? And what was the loud noise? It sounded like an explosion.

I don't know the answer to any of your questions. The first time I had the dream, I woke up as soon as I started down the hallway. Corban studied her furrowed brow. *We need answers.*

They stared into each other's eyes for a minute, their thoughts working overtime.

We should talk to Mom. Nikki gnawed her lower lip.

Yes, Solona can probably figure it out. At the thought of his mother-in-law, Corban experienced another surge of guilt.

Something you're not telling me? There was no avoiding the anger in her tone.

Corban decided a full confession would be the safest response. *Solona told me to share any premonitions about the colony with her.*

So she needed to know about this one right away?

Corban flinched. *Not necessarily. The first time I had this dream, I was the only one in it. I was searching for you in the storm. I didn't see anyone else inside the fort.*

But I was involved because you were shouting for me. Nikki threw aside the quilt and got to her feet. "Get dressed. We're going to see Mom."

***

"Let me see if I understand." Solona was seated behind the desk in the office of Brida's infirmary. "Sergey said Brida had been evacuated, and Linnea said they had to be ready, although you have no idea what they were expecting. Isaac said he was there to watch but couldn't see after the rain started. What was he watching for? There were other people in the apartment, but you don't know who."

Nikki nodded.

"And then you heard an explosion in the distance, and Sergey shouted for everyone to get to the roof?" Solona asked.

Corban nodded. "Unless I have this dream again, that's all we know."

"What do you think it means, Mom?" Nikki asked.

Solona pursed her lips and studied the ceiling for a minute. "All we know for certain is that this happens during the storm. We have two months to figure out what it means. I'm more concerned about where Nikki was during all this. Why were you two in Fort Brida? Linnea mentioned I was there too, but why?"

Corban shook his head. "I have no idea."

"It's also possible this doesn't take place during the next storm," Solona said. "It might happen several storms from now, since Corban admitted sometimes his premonitions show things far into the future." She flashed a mischievous grin. "The baby, for example."

Nikki glared at Corban. "You told her?"

He shook his head. "It wasn't me."

"Relax, Jing told me," Solona said. "And since she got it secondhand from Thane, a lot got lost in translation. You want to share it with me?"

"No," Nikki said at the exact moment Corban said, "Yes."

Nikki seized his hand. *Not now, please.*

"All right, if you're doing the mind-reading thing, as Jing calls it, I must've upset you. I'm sorry. You can tell me when you're ready." Solona stood, came around the desk, and ushered them toward the door. "Let me think about the storm premonition. You two should get back to Lakeside."

"That's it?" Nikki asked on the threshold. "You're not worried?"

"I'm too busy to be worried," Solona said. "I've got six merging Talents experiments planned for today. We'll talk later." She closed the door on them.

"I don't understand your mother," Corban said.

"I've never understood her." Nikki grasped his hand gentler this time. *But she's a genius, and I trust her judgment. She'll figure it out before we do.*

I hope so. Corban paused. *Are you sure you don't want to tell her about the baby premonition?*

No, I want to have a word with Jing about keeping her big mouth shut.

Let it go, Corban thought, *don't forget she's your sister-in-law now.*

Nikki sighed. *She was easier to handle when she was just my friend.*

EIGHTEEN
CRACKS

We don't need your help to cull the night terror lair near Lakeside tomorrow morning. Derek's message to Thane at the end of the work day was mysterious. *Bjoeren's figured out a way to destroy the den without putting any hunters in harm's way.*

Thane puzzled over the vague message as he went home to shower and change, and then headed to the dining hall.

The mystery was solved as he sat down to dinner with his three favorite people.

"We made Molotov cocktails today." Jing was attempting to appear nonchalant, but her dimpled grin spoiled the effect.

"How many?" Thane asked.

Corban and Nikki were also grinning across the table from him. "Fifteen," Corban said. "And Guild Master Bjoeren picked them up before we closed the shop."

"How are the hunters planning to use them?" Thane asked.

Jing was almost bursting to share the news. "By tying them to heavy arrows, lighting them, and launching

167

them at the lair from a safe distance!"

"Bjoeren only needs the hunters skilled with cross-bows," Corban said. "With his vision Talent, he thinks it'll be easy to eliminate the entire pack."

"That's genius," Thane said. "I wish we'd done it for the first hunt. Guild Master Evans and his daughter might still be alive."

The other three appeared uncomfortable at this announcement, and Thane felt a pang of guilt for spoiling the festive mood. "Sorry."

Nikki broke the awkward silence. "I'm grateful you and Corban won't need to help the hunters anymore."

"You're the one who figured out how to make the bottle bombs, so you should get all the credit," Corban said.

Nikki blushed and exchanged a knowing smile with Corban, and Thane felt a spark of envy at the effortless way they communicated without words. There were times when Thane wished he could read Jing's mind, but he noticed his wife had matured since the wedding three months ago. She hadn't cried once since the night they eloped, so he considered that real progress. Life was good.

***

Thane woke early and listened to the hunt from the comfort of his sitting room. He counted the explosions, confident there'd be no more night terrors outside Lakeside's gates after today. *One problem solved.*

He got dressed for work and kissed Jing goodbye before she was awake. "Love you, *meili*."

"Wuzz Thanzz?" Her sleepy mutters were as incoherent as Corban's.

Thane chuckled and left for the smithy.

As he pumped the bellows, heating the coals to forge the day's projects, Corban's latest premonition intruded on his thoughts. Thane made an effort to push it to the back of his mind. He knew he couldn't control things that threatened Vesta's survival, such as the annual hurricane-force storm, so he immersed himself in work, focusing on the sword he'd begun the day before.

"Thane?" Bertram used to tap him on the shoulder, but once he realized Thane heard him over the clanging of hammers on anvils, he spoke at a normal volume. "I have an assignment for you."

Thane raised the visor on his welding mask. He plunged the sword blade into the water bucket. "Yes, sir?"

"You can leave it for tomorrow. The Mechanics Guild master needs you at the dam to repair one of the turbines."

"I don't know anything about turbines." Thane pulled off his gloves and wiped the sweat from his forehead.

"That's why Zhao's going to meet you there." Bertram grinned. "Take whatever you need."

Thane was confused but didn't argue as he found a tool bag and began loading equipment for a welding repair. *Zhao's an herbalist now, so why would the mechanics request him? Why would Waterfall request me when the Smiths Guild's barracks is right there in the fort?*

Thane knew it was useless to speculate. Sometimes guild masters made odd requests. Solona Zegarelli, in particular, came up with assignments that defied explanation. He suspected she was behind this one.

"You can take the truck," Bertram said when Thane was ready to leave.

Thane nodded, picked up the heavy tool bag in both hands, and headed out of the smithy. A truck so rusty its original color was unidentifiable was parked near the marketplace park. He put the tools in the bed, shut the tailgate, climbed into the driver's seat, and started the engine.

Of all the vehicles he'd driven, this one sounded the worst. Thane doubted the ailing, ancient machine would make it to Lakeside's gates, much less navigate the eleven kilometers to Waterfall. He put the truck in gear but hesitated to press the accelerator until the engine quieted.

The rattling grew louder. With a sigh, he stepped on the pedal, and the vehicle shuddered and sputtered a moment before the wheels began to turn.

An hour later, he drove across the hydroelectric dam and parked outside Waterfall's main gates. "Where can I find the Mechanics Guild master?" he asked the sentry on duty, an older woman who looked so similar to Robin Aziz that she must've been Robin's mother.

She pointed to a door next to the sentries' office marked *No Entry—Keep Out.* "Down there."

Thane opened the heavy door and eyed a dimly lit spiral staircase with trepidation. He gripped his tool bag and started downward. After a few meters, the air grew humid and the metal grating of the stairs became slick with condensation. He heard the roar of falling water beyond the concrete wall to his left and wondered how the manmade structure was built to take advantage of the Cold River's natural plunge.

How did they divert the river while they constructed it? And how did they bring in all the cement? Thane hadn't seen a working crane in his lifetime. He considered himself the least qualified metal-smith to repair a turbine but resolved to see for himself what was wrong with the dam.

He shifted the bag to his right shoulder, freeing his

left hand to grasp the railing. He made sure his right foot was secure before lowering his damaged left leg to the next step. It was slow going, but he didn't want to fall down twelve flights of stairs. *It's a nice day for a descent into the bowels of Vesta.*

The temperature of the stairwell dropped with each level, until Thane's teeth were chattering. *And no one told me to bring a jacket. This is the worst assignment I've ever had, and I don't even know what work needs to be done.*

Ten meters later, the stairs ended at a wide concrete platform, which extended seventy meters to a natural stone wall. Five concrete cylinders, each three meters high and eight meters in diameter, were spaced along the platform. The whirring sounds combined with the roar of the waterfall were almost deafening. He knew there was a turbine inside each cylinder but didn't know how to access the massive machines.

Thane started down the platform, grateful to be off the slippery stairs. At the third turbine, he discovered a fifty-something man in black coveralls, his back to Thane, removing the screws on a one-meter square access panel the exact putty color of the damp concrete.

"Hello?" He tapped the man on the shoulder, causing him to yelp and drop his screwdriver.

The mechanic turned to face Thane. He had bushy gray eyebrows and a white mustache but not one hair on his shiny brown dome. "Who are you? How did you get down here?"

Thane pointed to his tool bag. "I was sent to help with a repair. Are you the guild master?"

The man gestured to his earplugs, bent to retrieve the screwdriver, and turned back to the access panel without another word.

"Sir, can you hear me?" Thane asked louder.

"We heard you." Zhao walked into view around the curve of the cylinder. He was wearing a tool belt around his hips instead of a yellow herbalist's apron. Isaac Nomura was right behind him, a large solar flashlight in one hand.

Thane shook hands with his brother-in-law and former roommate. "Doesn't the noise hurt your ears?"

"Wool batting." Zhao pointed to his ears.

Isaac nodded, indicating his own plugged ears. "Mutes it a little, but we can hear, unlike Guild Master Moul." He nodded toward the mechanic.

"Frieda's dad?" Thane asked.

"Her uncle, I think." Zhao tapped Moul on the shoulder, startling him a second time. "What do you need us to do?" he shouted into one of the guild master's plugged ears.

Moul held up a finger in the universal sign for "just a minute" and finished removing the last screw from the panel. He gripped the edges and pulled it free, then gestured for Thane, Zhao, and Isaac to take a look.

Zhao and Isaac stood shoulder to shoulder and went on tiptoe to see inside, but Thane could see over the tops of their heads. The interior of the cylinder was filled with a cone-shaped machine made of interlocking steel paddles. It was motionless. Thane noticed the water rushing beneath the open circular floor, flowing around the paddles, which should've been spinning. At least, he assumed that was how it worked.

"I hope he doesn't expect us to climb inside. How are you supposed to help?" Thane asked Zhao. "There's at least fifty people in the guild, but they requested an ex-mechanic? And what qualifications do you have?" He turned to Isaac.

"No professional skills." Isaac shrugged. "We're obviously not here to do a repair."

"Using our Talents was Solona's idea." Zhao reached inside and brushed his fingers over one of the motionless paddles.

Thane had the urge to yank Zhao's arm back but forced himself to remain calm. *It's not going to suddenly start spinning and chop off his arm.*

"No one's touched this for at least forty storms." Zhao stepped away from the access hole and turned to Thane with a frown. "Solona wanted me to make sure no one tampered with it."

"Who would do something like that?" Thane was uneasy at the thought of sabotage, but he recognized the wisdom in investigating the possibility. "Stray-haters, like my slime worm uncle?"

Zhao's expression was grim. "Fort Brida's just below the dam. You can't tell me the building site was a coincidence."

A block of ice formed in Thane's stomach. "Even dead, Leighton's still a threat."

"Which is why Solona asked us to check." Isaac turned to Thane and Zhao. "I don't see anything unusual inside the turbine chamber. It's not jammed, and the gears aren't rusty. I think the motor's worn out, and I'll bet the other turbines aren't going to last much longer."

"Machines weren't meant to run without maintenance for forty storms," Zhao said. "Not that I blame the Mechanics Guild. Tools wear out, and there's no way to replace them."

"Does he know you're searching for evidence of tampering?" Thane tilted his head in Moul's direction.

"I doubt it," Zhao said. "When I was in the guild, he came down here after each storm to check for structural problems."

Moul observed them with mild interest but did nothing. He seemed to assume the three Strays could fix whatever needed fixing.

"Corban said the lights flickered each time he attended a mayors' meeting in Waterfall. How long ago do you think it stopped working?" Thane asked.

Zhao shrugged. "If Moul only checks the turbines after each storm, it might've been like this for ten months."

"Not good. Is one broken turbine going to compromise the power grid?" Isaac asked.

"It generates power, but without a way to divert the water to the other four turbines, the pressure's been building beneath us"—Zhao gave Thane and Isaac a serious look—"which is why Solona wanted us here. I did my part. Now it's your turn."

"Right." Isaac switched on his flashlight and directed the large beam at the top of the fifty-meter concrete wall. "I'll need some time."

"Me too." Thane shut his eyes and focused his hearing, filtering out the noise of the waterfall, the other turbines, and the hum of the unseen generators. He didn't know what to listen for, so it took several minutes, but when he detected a different sound, he knew what it was.

There was a subtle creaking beneath the central cylinder, indicating a flaw had formed, and it was growing. Without opening his eyes, he turned his face toward the high concrete wall and concentrated on locating the same noise. He heard the creaking, but it wasn't a single flaw, and it wasn't subtle.

"I hear cracks in the concrete. They'll spread, like a chip in a pane of glass, extending until the pressure from the water becomes too strong for it to stand." Thane opened his eyes and exchanged a worried frown with Zhao.

Together they turned to watch Isaac, who was playing the light slowly over each section of the dam. He was squinting, his mouth pinched in concentration.

Thane, Zhao, and Guild Master Moul waited in silence, watching Isaac.

Five minutes later, Isaac turned off the flashlight and announced in a strained voice, "We're in trouble."

"Cracks?" Thane asked.

Isaac nodded. "Big ones."

"Cracks," Zhao said. "And no way to repair them without cement and rebar—"

"Scaffolding," Isaac added, "and a crane—"

"Tools we don't have." Zhao swore and gestured for Moul to replace the access panel. The mechanic shrugged and got to work.

"When do you think it'll give way?" Thane asked.

"I guess we have until the next storm," Zhao said.

Thane felt a chill as he thought of Corban's premonition. "We'd better report to Solona and Derek."

***

Zhao knew where to find them. "They'll be in the infirmary. They're always in the infirmary." He climbed into the passenger's seat of the Smiths Guild truck, with Isaac in the middle.

"Thanks for carrying the tool bag for me." Thane's bad leg ached from the arduous ascent up the slick spiral staircase, but he'd managed, thanks to his brother-in-law's generous assistance. He started the engine, wincing at the racket. "Are they still experimenting with merging Talents?"

"You're welcome," Zhao said. "Yes, they've been

experimenting, but I'm exempt. They haven't found anyone with a Talent like mine. I'm surprised they haven't summoned you yet."

"Who says they haven't?" Thane put the truck in gear and drove the five kilometers of rutted, washed-out gravel roads to Fort Brida.

"Sometimes I think walking would be faster," Isaac said as Thane drove through the open gates into the courtyard.

"Sometimes I think the colony needs a chiropractor." Thane parked near the infirmary and climbed out of the cab with a sigh of relief. With no shock absorbers in the aging vehicle, the thirty minute drive was painful.

"Nehal Hong could adjust your back," Zhao said.

"No, thanks. Corban told me about her physical therapy regimen. I think his kindest word was *torture*."

Zhao laughed and opened the door to the infirmary. There was no one at the round table in the front office, so he led Thane and Isaac to the door on the other side of the room. Zhao knocked but didn't wait for an answer before walking in.

Thane was right on his heels but paused when he realized they were barging in on a practice session. He hooked Zhao's elbow with one hand and Isaac's with the other, holding them back. Derek and Solona stood near the left-hand wall, and Solona put a finger to her lips, warning the young men not to speak.

Linnea Savoy, Sergey Gupta, Robin Aziz, and a dark-skinned young man Thane didn't recognize were sitting cross-legged on the floor, two on each side of the single hospital bed in the middle of the room. Each Stray focused his or her gaze on the bed.

"On three," Solona said. "One, two—"

Before she uttered "three," the bed rose like a

rocket toward the ceiling but stopped before the head-board crashed into the overhead light.

Thane held his breath, watching in fascination as the bed began to rotate like a fan blade in midair, spinning faster and faster until it was a blur.

"And down," Derek said.

The spinning ceased, and the bed plunged toward the floor but stopped millimeters from the wood planks before coming to rest gently on four legs.

Thane waited to see if the experiment was over before exhaling.

"Well done," Solona said.

Sergey shook his head. "I think we can do more. Linnea and I have been practicing." He flashed her a flustered grin. "What I mean is we've discovered something new about merging our Talents. Let's try moving the bed again, and this time we'll need more weight."

"Yes, let's try it," Linnea said. "Thane, Zhao, Isaac, come sit on the bed."

Thane's jaw dropped, but Zhao nodded. "Come on," he said, "it's safe."

"As long as you don't do the spinning thing." Thane reluctantly followed Zhao and Isaac. "And I'm tall, so I'd appreciate it if you didn't put my head through the ceiling."

He took a seat near the foot of the bed, while Zhao and Isaac sat back-to-back near the headboard. Thane gripped the footboard with one hand, trying not to appear nervous as the four telekinetic Strays focused on the bed. This time Sergey and Robin held hands, and Linnea and the other young man did the same.

"Ready?" Solona said. "On three. One, two—"

Thane set his jaw, expecting to receive a concussion, but the bed rose a meter off the floor and stopped. This time it rotated slowly, giving him a three-hundred-sixty degree view of the room before returning to the floor.

"Good job!" Derek clapped and everyone in the room joined in.

"Holding hands makes a big difference," Linnea said. "I felt Kabir's Talent flowing through me. I know it sounds strange—"

"No, it doesn't," Thane said. "Corban and Nikki told us being in contact seems to enhance their Talents. Nikki's Talent only works with contact, but it didn't take long for her to start sensing emotions, like Corban does."

"Linnea and I have been experimenting on our own." Sergey's eyes found Linnea's, and she gave him a nod to continue. "When we hold hands, our Talents seem stronger."

"We moved a truck!" Linnea seemed quite eager to share this. "Uphill, with the brakes on!"

"Darkness," Derek said. "You've practiced on your own?"

"You moved a truck? We need to investigate this further." Solona grinned. "Let's try moving—"

"No," Robin interrupted. "I'm done for today. I need to nurse Solona."

"What?" Thane shot a confused look at Nikki's mother, earning some laughter from the others. "Oh, you mean your baby. *That* Solona." He got to his feet and offered Robin a hand up from the floor.

"Thanks," she said.

"We should go too." Sergey walked around the bed to offer Linnea a hand. "Linnea gets a headache if we practice too long."

Linnea thanked Sergey with a dazzling smile, which left no doubt in Thane's mind how they felt about each other. Sergey slipped an arm around Linnea's waist, and they followed Robin to the door.

"We want to practice with a team of six tomorrow," Derek called after them.

"Six?" the other Strays echoed.

"We're going to need more space," Kabir said.

"Good point," Solona said. "Let's meet at the gates at midday and walk down to the river. I think you've practiced long enough with solid mass."

"Liquid?" Thane arched an eyebrow at Solona.

She flashed him a mischievous grin before escorting the telekinetics to the door. Closing the door after Kabir, she turned to Thane, Zhao, and Isaac. "Any evidence of tampering?"

"No, ma'am," Zhao said. "It stopped working all by itself."

Solona turned to Thane. "What did you hear?"

"A crack in the foundation, beneath the frozen turbine." He nodded at Derek's troubled expression. "And more cracks in the dam, and they're expanding."

"What did you see?" Solona asked Isaac.

"Lots of cracks in the wall," he replied. "I lost count after twenty. They're big and they're expanding, like Thane said."

"We need to fix the dam," Zhao said. "That's obvious."

"But how to do it isn't so obvious," Thane added. "We'd need a working crane and lots of cement, but Vesta has neither."

"The mechanics can shut off the water to the turbines for short intervals, but we don't want the river flooding its banks upstream. That would be bad for West Fort and Lakeside," Derek said.

Thane tried to think. "What happens to the dam during a storm? Do they just let the turbines run?"

"There's a water release gate near the top of the dam.

It's opened for storms so the excess water doesn't overwhelm the system," Zhao said.

"It won't be enough to relieve the pressure," Isaac said. "The next storm might be its last."

Thane frowned as he thought of Corban's premonition. "Brida should be evacuated. Without a way to repair the cracks, it's not safe."

Solona and Derek exchanged a troubled glance. "Yes, safety first," Derek said.

"But—?" Thane prodded.

"But we'll have to figure out where to send everyone," Derek said. "We're comfortable here. Sending people back to where they used to live will be met with resistance from Survivors."

"Finding housing will be a challenge," Solona added. "But without a way to repair the cracks and the turbine, we don't have a choice."

"We'll get started on a plan right away." Derek didn't sound optimistic, but he turned to Thane, Zhao, and Isaac with a wary smile. "Please don't share this information with anyone yet. We don't want to cause a panic."

Solona turned away before Thane saw her expression. He wanted to ask her if she thought the cracks were related to Corban's latest premonition but stopped himself. Corban had disclosed his updated version of the storm dream to Nikki and Thane but no one else. Thane hadn't even mentioned it to Jing. *Knowing the future is a terrible burden.*

"Right, we don't want to cause a panic." Thane turned to Zhao with an awkward grin. "I guess you could move in with Jing and me."

Zhao rolled his eyes. "Only as a last resort!"

NINETEEN
TRAVIS'S WARNING

Eliana dropped by the apothecary in the morning. She had Travis on one hip, and he was bawling at the top of his lungs.

Nikki came around the counter and attempted to greet her nephew with a kiss on his chubby pink cheek, but he twisted his face away from her. "No!"

"I'm guessing this isn't a social visit?" Nikki arched an eyebrow at her sister.

"I need a break." Eliana set Travis on his unsteady feet; he'd started pulling up a week ago. "Mom's at the hospital today, assisting Dr. DeKalb with an appendectomy, so I don't have a babysitter."

Jing exited the lab and walked over to join them. She offered Travis a wooden ball, but he bellowed, "No!" and clung to his mother's legs.

"Could I leave him here with you for a few hours while I get a haircut and maybe a nap in your apartment?"

Nikki studied her sister's pale face and the dark circles beneath her eyes. "Sure, Jing and I can watch him. Are you all right?"

"No." Eliana pushed her tangled auburn bangs out of her eyes. "I'm pregnant."

Jing and Nikki gasped in unison. "That's wonderful!" Jing said.

Eliana waved away their congratulations. "I wasn't this sick with Travis. Mom thinks I might be carrying twins."

Nikki gaped at her. "Darkness! Twins! Why didn't you tell us sooner?"

"Because I haven't been able to get out of bed for a month. Derek's aunt Blythe has been kind enough to babysit Travis for me. This is the first day I've had to manage him by myself since the morning sickness hit."

"Where's Blythe today?" Nikki asked.

"She's got a cold. Probably worn out from taking care of Travis. And Derek couldn't take him because he's at a meeting with Greenfield's mayor. He's trying to convince her to send us more food in exchange for whatever he thinks Brida can produce."

"His merchant skills at work," Nikki said. "He told me he wanted to get back to trading as soon as construction was finished on Brida."

Before Eliana could respond, her eyes widened, and she put a hand to her mouth. "Bathroom!"

Nikki and Jing watched her sprint toward the examination room and its tiny half bath. Travis let out a howl and tried to crawl after his mother, but Jing scooped him up. "It's all right."

Travis wouldn't be consoled until Eliana emerged from the back. She looked worse than before she vomited, her steps slow and unsteady.

"Get her a chair," Jing told Nikki. "I'll make some ginger tea." She set Travis's diapered bottom on the floor and hurried to the compounding lab.

Nikki found a folding chair behind the counter.

Once Eliana was seated, Nikki tried to get Travis interested in the ball, but he clung to his mother's legs and screamed as if someone was sawing off one of his limbs.

"See what you have to look forward to?" Eliana rolled her eyes at Nikki. "'Get busy and make babies,' Mom said."

Nikki ignored her sister's feeble attempt at humor. "Do you think he senses his siblings? Maybe he's already jealous?"

"He's ten months old, so he doesn't say much. It's hard to tell what's bothering him." Eliana stroked her son's thick hair, which grew in tight spirals like Derek's but was auburn like his mother's and grandmother's. "He's good for Blythe. He didn't start shrieking like this until early this morning, when he woke up and realized he was stuck with me, I guess."

Nikki frowned. "Are you sure there's not more to it? Remember Travis was inconsolable when the *Unity* was about to land? He sensed it before anyone knew it was coming. We were already getting a glimpse of his potential Talent."

"You think he senses something now?" Eliana bit her lip.

Nikki sat on the floor next to Travis and tentatively extended a hand toward him. "You know, I've never held him since the day he was born. I never touch him except to give him quick kisses. Maybe I can see what he senses. If he had a premonition, I might see something in his memories." She locked eyes with her sister. "If it's all right with you."

Eliana nodded. "It's worth a try."

Jing emerged from the compounding lab with a steaming cup of ginger tea. "I added some peppermint too." She handed Eliana the cup and got quiet when she noticed what Nikki was about to do.

Nikki placed her hand on her nephew's small back. His memories filled her mind, and she struggled to make sense of them. Simple images took shape and vanished as fast as they appeared: familiar faces, especially Eliana's, Derek's, Solona's, and Blythe's; the Grahams' apartment in Fort Brida; his favorite toys; his favorite foods; trees and fields. He remembered a night filled with the sounds of gunfire, when the sentries culled the night terrors outside the fort, but one image persisted, more prominent than the others: a simple view of the blue sky with Ilios shining overhead.

Nikki focused on this memory, watching as Ilios drifted behind iron-gray clouds. The clouds grew, filling the sky until all the blue was blotted out. It took all of her self-control not to gasp so she wouldn't alarm Travis. She snatched her hand away. "It's the storm. He senses that it's coming."

"It's not due for two months," Eliana said. "Not until his birthday."

"If he's this upset, I think it'll be here soon." Nikki got to her feet. "Since the satellite's been offline, we've had no way of knowing when the storm will hit. A few extra hours' notice is a real blessing." She tried not to let the fear show on her face as she recalled Corban's premonition about the storm. *Sergey said Brida was evacuated. And then there was the explosion.* She didn't understand what it all meant, or why she and Corban were there during the storm.

"Time to put the communication teams to work." Jing headed toward the door. "I'll see who's at the sentries' station."

"Tell them Brida needs to be evacuated!" Nikki said.

"What?" Eliana asked. "What are you talking about?"

"Why?" Jing turned to Nikki with a startled expression.

"Because something's going to happen during the storm." Nikki took a deep breath. "Corban had a premonition."

"How long have you known about this?" Eliana asked.

"I just found out, and we told Mom a week ago." Nikki wasn't sure what else to share with them about the premonition especially since she didn't understand it herself. "All I know is Fort Brida's not safe during the storm."

Travis erupted into fresh, earsplitting wails.

"Shh." Eliana tried without success to soothe him, but Nikki figured he was responding to her sister's heightened stress level.

"What should we do?" Jing shouted to be heard over Travis's shrieks.

"Tell the communications team to let Derek know Brida has to be evacuated," Nikki said. "We may only have a few hours."

"Zhao's at Brida!" There was a note of panic in Jing's voice. "I'll be right back." She raced out the door.

"There are things I need from the apartment." Eliana bounced Travis in her arms, but it didn't soothe him.

"There's nothing you can't live without." Nikki didn't mean to sound harsh, but her sister appeared to be in shock. Nikki took the ring of keys out of her apron pocket and unhooked the one to her apartment. She dropped it into Eliana's palm. "Go. Make yourself comfortable. You can use my new kitchen towels for diapers, if you need to."

Eliana got to her feet. "What about Derek? And Mom?"

"I'm sure they'll have to supervise the evacuation."

Eliana opened her mouth to protest, so Nikki added a stern, "There's nothing you can do. I need to secure the inventory here. Barricade the apartment windows, if you feel up to it. I'm sure a neighbor would be willing to help when they hear that the storm is coming."

Nikki didn't wait for her sister and nephew to leave before hurrying back to the compounding lab. Twin stacks of nested shipping containers in assorted sizes, with *Unity* printed on the lids, were piled floor to ceiling next to the commercial-sized dehydrator. *Good idea saving these, Mom.* She grabbed some boxes and went back to the shop to pack up the apothecary's inventory.

Normally the shop lost dozens of jars during a storm because there wasn't enough time to secure everything. Travis's early warning Talent was a priceless gift that would save lives and property. Nikki knew there was nothing she could do to help with the evacuation, but it didn't stop her from worrying. She focused on securing the shop and tried not to think about Corban's premonition.

She started on the most labor-intensive herbs first, the essential oils. Some of the steel boxes contained leftover packing materials inside, making it easy to protect the tiny brown bottles from each other. She'd just finished snapping a lid on the oils container when Jing returned, breathing hard.

"All set. There was a message-sender on duty, so the warning will go out to all the forts. And I went by the smithy to tell Thane."

"What about Corban?" Nikki picked up a box and started on the shelf above the essential oils display.

"He's still at Solona's rooftop garden." Jing grabbed an empty box and started packing the contents of a lower shelf. "I'm sure he'll notice the commotion and come straight here."

The bell over the apothecary entrance tinkled. Nikki didn't pause in her work as she turned her head to greet the customer with a cautious smile. "How can we help you, Ms. Vandermeer?"

"I was checking to see if Solona was in today, but I guess not. What in darkness are you doing?"

"Packing the shop," Jing said. "The storm's coming."

Ms. Vandermeer turned to gape at the bright blue sky through the door. "It's not due for two months! How do you know?"

"My nephew can sense things before they happen." Nikki didn't like the way this conversation was going. "Can we help you with something?"

"Your nephew's a Stray?" Ms. Vandermeer scowled.

"Second-generation. He's more attuned to danger than my husband, Corban Abrams, who has a Talent for clairvoyance."

"How old is your nephew?"

"Ten months. He was born during the last storm."

"You're preparing for the storm over the advice of an *infant*?"

Nikki stopped what she was doing and gave the Survivor a cold look. "Yes. Travis sensed the *Unity* coming before it touched down. He was a few weeks old when it happened."

"Did you come here for a remedy, or did you just want to harass us?" Jing asked.

"You can't talk to me like that!" Ms. Vandermeer snapped. "I'm going to complain to Mayor Brooks. You two are rude and reckless, and a worthless Stray has no business managing the apothecary."

"You do that." Jing's tone turned cold. "Be sure to tell the mayor her children are worthless Strays too, and see how she responds."

"Bigot," Nikki hissed the moment the door shut behind Ms. Vandermeer. "She's holding a grudge as if it's our fault her daughter's infertile from the vaccine. She'll be the first to complain when the storm hits and she's not prepared."

The sky remained blue when Nikki and Jing finished arranging all the boxes on the floor, the entire glass contents of the shop and compounding lab secure. They went outside to close the shutters and saw the other marketplace vendors rushing around, boarding up huts, taking down tents and awnings, and boxing up their merchandise.

"I'm glad they took the warning seriously," Jing said.

"What's happening? The whole fort's in commotion." Corban parted the crowds to reach the apothecary's porch, carrying fabric bags full of the juniper berries and ginger roots he'd harvested.

Nikki didn't mince words. "The storm's coming. Travis warned us."

Corban's jaw dropped. "But it's too soon! Brida's supposed to be evacuated!"

"The message went out two hours ago." Jing snatched the bags from his hands and set them on the floor inside the door. "Grab the hammer and help us secure the shop." She locked the glass-paneled door to the apothecary and focused her efforts on the heavy wooden door next to it. This storm door was on a track so it could be rolled in front of the entrance, but Jing wasn't able to budge it. The track and wheels were rusted.

"Wait a minute, and we'll help," Nikki said.

Jing shook her head. "Finish the window. We need Thane's muscles." She dashed off toward the smithy without waiting for a reply.

The moment Jing was out of sight, Corban turned to Nikki. "We need to go to Brida and help them evacuate!"

"I'm sure Mom and Derek have it under control." Nikki gripped his shoulder. *Calm down. We'd just be in the way at Brida.*

But my premonition!

Nikki couldn't remember seeing Corban this scared since the moment they'd been standing on the wide bridge, waiting for the *Unity* to explode. *Calm down. I don't know what's going to happen. I can't think about it right now, not when we have work to do.*

She shook her head and turned back to wrestling the shutter into place over the front window. The wood was bowed from age and weather, leaving a few centimeters of glass unprotected.

Corban added his weight to the warped panel, flattening it until he was able to secure the iron latch that held it closed. He snatched up a hammer and a fistful of nails from the porch. "We should find places to shelter the Strays here in Lakeside."

Nikki realized Corban was making an effort to sound calm, but his expression wasn't convincing. His face was pale and his lips were pinched into a thin line.

"There's not enough time." She kept her hands pressed against the uncooperative shutter to keep it from bowing while Corban nailed the corners to secure it. She thought about Ms. Vandermeer's reaction to the storm warning. "I doubt people would be willing to share their apartments. The Strays have to take shelter at the landing strip."

"Are there enough trucks to get them to the ships?" Corban moved to the storm door, grasped the rusty handle with both hands, and pulled hard, but it didn't move.

"I don't know." Nikki added her strength to the door. They dug in their heels, but it was no use. "We need Thane, and maybe Bertram, to get this to move." She gave up and leaned back against the door, panting.

"We have to do something." Corban pounded the uncooperative door with his fist. "I shouldn't have waited so long to tell Solona about my premonition!"

"You can't control the weather." Nikki seized his wrist before he punched the door again. *You can't blame yourself for what you foresee. Let's focus on what we can do right now. You can wallow in guilt later.*

Corban gave a reluctant nod.

Nikki spotted Thane and Jing navigating the marketplace chaos to reach them. *The four of us should be able to move this door. Then let's go to the landing strip and help Strays board the ships.* She sensed that he was attempting to control his anxiety, and realized she needed to do the same.

TWENTY
EVACUATION

Corban knew he should take Nikki's advice and feel guilty later, but the growing sense of foreboding made his stomach churn, as if he were about to face a night terror unarmed. *Calm down.* He repeated Nikki's advice like a mantra, but his pounding heart didn't seem to be getting the message.

He climbed into the back of a Cooks Guild truck with Thane, Nikki, and Jing. The bed was loaded with crates of food and supplies for people taking refuge in the ships. The other forts would send whatever supplies they could spare, if there was time. Corban stared at the gathering gray clouds and prayed there would be enough time.

"What about our apartment?" Jing asked Thane.

"Zhao can secure it." Thane sat on a *Unity* box filled with toiletries, his back to the cab.

"But Zhao's at Brida!" Jing sat cross-legged next to Thane on a cooler that gave off a strong smell of fish.

"Not for long, *meili.* Derek told me Zhao's on his way here, so I left the apartment unlocked for him."

"What about Derek and Solona?" Corban sat on a

wheelhouse, the one free spot he could find.

"We won't know unless Derek sends one of us a message." Thane bit his lip. "I'm sure they'll evacuate as soon as everyone's out."

Nikki perched on a huge bag of potatoes next to Corban. "But we know some people won't be leaving, and somehow Corban and I will be there when the storm breaks."

"I think you need to tell me about this premonition." Jing frowned at Corban. "I seem to be the only one who has no idea what you're talking about."

Corban described his latest dream to the other three, concluding with, "There are missing details, like always. I don't know what I heard in the distance. Some kind of explosion."

Jing opened her mouth to say something, but Thane spoke first, his tone somber. "You heard the dam collapsing. Fort Brida's going to be flooded."

"*What?*" Nikki and Jing gasped in unison.

Corban gaped at his brother. "How do you know?"

"I know because Zhao, Isaac, and I inspected a broken turbine inside the dam, on Solona's orders"—Thane took a deep breath—"two days ago."

"Two days?" Jing clamped a hand over her mouth.

Thane wrapped an arm around Jing's shoulders. "We suspect the central turbine hasn't worked since the last storm. I heard a crack in the foundation beneath it and more cracks in the main wall. Isaac saw cracks in the wall, and he said they're expanding. We discussed the possibility of the dam giving way during the next storm."

"And now the storm's here." Corban struggled to get enough air into his lungs.

"Solona thought we had two months to evacuate Brida," Thane said, "but now we have less than two hours, if we're lucky."

One look at the darkening sky ratcheted up Corban's sense of foreboding.

Nikki grasped his hand. *It's not your fault the storm's early.*

It's my fault we're not prepared!

Stop thinking like that! We can't turn back time. Let's decide what we can *do now to salvage the situation.* To Thane and Jing, Nikki said, "Who knows about the dam besides Mom, Derek, Isaac, Zhao, and the four of us?"

"Derek asked us not to tell anyone yet because he didn't want to cause a panic," Thane said.

Corban grimaced. "Can we panic now?"

"No." Nikki squeezed his hand, hard. "Brida's being evacuated. With Frieda Moul shouting Derek's orders, no one's going to wonder if this is some kind of emergency drill."

"Vesta's never had an emergency drill that I can recall," Thane said.

Frustration crept into Nikki's tone. "My point is the Strays can take refuge in the ships. They'll be safe when the dam breaks. I'm sure we'll see truckloads of people arriving at the landing strip, so let's see what we can do to help."

"What about Sergey, Linnea, Isaac, and the others? What were they doing in Brida? Why on the north wall?" Jing asked. "And why did they need to go up on the roof after the explosion?"

"Brida's north wall faces upriver, so it's the closest one to the dam. I'd guess they're on the third floor to try to get above the water." Corban gasped as the final piece of the puzzle fell into place. "They're going to use their Talents to try to stop the flood!"

"It's impossible!" Jing said. "There's no way they can

stop a wall of water!"

"They'll drown!" Nikki gripped Corban's arm. *We have to convince them not to risk their lives!*

Corban felt a chill. *Maybe that's why we're in Brida.*

But we'll be too late, Nikki thought. *And where am I during all of this? How do we get separated?*

I don't know. Corban hated not knowing the beginning or the end of his premonition, and that they were attempting to carve out a plan based on speculation.

Jing made an impatient noise. "Anything you two need to share with us?"

Nikki shook her head. "We're trying to figure out the missing details."

Thane shot Corban a stern look. "If those details have anything to do with you and Nikki going to Brida, think again."

"We're going to the landing strip right now, aren't we?" Corban didn't mean to sound defensive, but he'd already made up his mind to keep Thane and Jing away from Fort Brida, even if it meant lying to them. *And I want to keep you safe too,* he thought.

I think we're in this together. Corban sensed Nikki's nervousness, but her determination pushed it aside. *We need to warn Sergey, Linnea, and the others not to attempt to stop the flood.*

I've never been able to change a premonition, Corban reminded her.

There's always a first time. Nikki took a deep breath. *As soon as we can slip away from Thane and Jing, we'll head to Brida.*

Corban didn't like anything about this so-called plan. *Assuming we're there when the flood hits, what do we hope to accomplish—besides drowning?*

Don't assume the worst. I don't know what we need to do, but we'll think of something when the time comes.

I wish I had your confidence.

This isn't confidence, Nikki thought, *this is barely contained panic.*

As the truck approached the wide bridge, Corban craned his neck to see what was happening at the landing strip.

Nineteen massive starships were parked permanently on both sides of the cracked tarmac, their rusting metal carcasses forming a ghost town. Three of the ships—the hospital, library, and Shrine—were put to regular use, but the other ships' primary purpose was to provide shelter from the annual storm.

The truck crossed the Cold River and reached the tarmac, and Corban's gaze was drawn to the remains of the twentieth ship, the *Unity*, halfway between the Shrine and the library. The huge pile of ash and blackened steel girders served as a grim reminder of a premonition that had haunted him for months. *If they'd listened, they'd be alive today. Your father, Jing's father, Fenton's father—*

It was their choice, Nikki thought. *Without your premonitions, many more would've died.*

You give me too much credit. Corban shook his head.

No, I don't. Your premonitions saved my life, and Jing's, and now you've saved the life of every Stray in Brida because no one would've known about the dam.

"You two need to stop that and pay attention." Jing's voice interrupted Corban's next thought. "It looks like this evacuation needs someone to take charge."

There were fifteen trucks parked on the tarmac and more were arriving every few minutes. At least one hundred colonists crowded the gangways of several ships, their arms loaded down with bedding, provisions, and, in a few cases, small children.

The driver of the Cooks Guild truck parked outside the library, where dozens of people were lined up on the gangway to the airlock.

"I guess no one knows the entry code." Corban wasn't surprised, since few colonists used the library.

"I've got this one." Jing pointed to the crowd outside the hospital. "Someone needs to tell them that the ship's not a storm refuge."

"I'll do it." Thane climbed down from the bed and offered Jing a hand.

Their truck driver, a big, burly man wearing a dainty purple apron, climbed from the cab. "Take a crate or a cooler to each ship." He reached over the side and grabbed the fish cooler Jing had used as a seat.

Thane nodded, lifted a crate from the bed, and placed it in Jing's arms. "Got it, *meili*?"

She nodded and headed toward the library. Thane hefted a second fish-scented cooler and headed toward the hospital.

"I'll take one to the *Courage*." Nikki pointed across the tarmac.

"I'll come with you. We should stay together." Corban helped Nikki down from the tailgate, handed her a crate, and picked up a cooler.

They started toward the half-rust, half-silver ship parked fifty meters from the library. Weeds and curling vines grew through the hundreds of cracks in the crumbling tarmac, threatening to trip them with every step, but the nagging sense of foreboding urged Corban to walk faster.

Nikki brushed elbows with him. *How are we going to sneak away?* She matched his pace, not even breathing hard. *Thane will hear us.*

I'm hoping he'll be too distracted to worry about us. Corban shifted the cooler to get a better grip.

Don't count on it. He always looks after his little brother.
Yes, but now he's responsible for Jing's safety.

Nikki shook her head. *I think it's the other way around. She looks after Thane.*

They reached the foot of the crowded gangway, and Corban noticed the airlock wasn't open. "The codes are the same on every ship!" he shouted to the man at the top of the ramp.

A familiar face turned to peer down at him. "What is it?" Fenton DeKalb called.

Dagmar DeKalb stood on tiptoe and grinned at Corban over Fenton's shoulder.

"Pi!" Nikki yelled. "The first six numbers of pi!"

Fenton turned back to the airlock controls. In a moment, the large round door cycled open, and everyone waiting on the gangway cheered.

Corban and Nikki followed the crowd up to the ship and placed the crate and cooler next to Dagmar in the entryway. "Flush out the cistern, so it'll be ready to collect fresh rainwater, and check the power," Corban told her. "If all the lights don't come on, check to see if the solar panels need to be cleaned. There should be a hatch on the bridge to reach them."

"Sounds dangerous, but thanks for the advice." Dagmar smiled. "And thank you for warning us to evacuate."

"You saved Thane's life during the internment, so I'd say we're even." Corban grabbed Nikki's hand and rushed her down the ramp without hearing Dagmar's reply.

The sense of urgency gnawed at Corban's insides. He and Nikki ran to the Cooks Guild truck and discovered the bed was already empty. He noticed five new trucks had arrived at the landing strip in the short time they'd been at the *Courage.* "It looks like the evacuation is going well."

Nikki pointed out two green trucks coming across the bridge. "Farmers Guild, so those are from Greenfield. Let's see if they have food to distribute."

Corban caught her arm before she started toward the nearest truck. *There are hundreds of people coming to the landing strip. They don't need our help.*

Nikki faced him, gnawing her lower lip. *You think we should go to Brida right now?*

I think there's a reason we were there in my premonition. He frowned at the sky, which was growing darker as the storm clouds blotted out Ilios. *And we don't have much time.*

What about Thane? Nikki turned toward the library ship. *He'll try to stop us.*

Not if we're careful not to speak aloud. He matched her gaze, watching for Thane to exit the library, but Nikki seemed too impatient to wait.

Let's move while he's preoccupied, like you said. She closed the tailgate, moved to the driver's side door, climbed into the cab, and started the engine.

Corban frowned but followed her lead, climbing into the passenger's side.

Nikki touched his hand before putting the vehicle in gear. *If anyone asks, we're driving to Brida for another load of evacuees.*

Corban stole another nervous glance at the hospital ship before nodding. He turned his head to check out the library's gangway, but there was no sign of Jing. He put a hand on Nikki's shoulder. *Let's hurry before they realize we're gone. How fast can you drive?*

Hang on. Nikki set her jaw and stepped on the accelerator.

***

The wind was beginning to pick up as they passed Waterfall. Corban turned in his seat to study the dam through the back window, but he was too far away to see the cracks he'd noticed a few months ago. *And I thought the cracks were normal.* Regret began to displace the guilt he felt. He watched until he lost sight of the dam through the trees.

Nikki didn't slow as she took the right fork toward Brida. He was tempted to warn her not to break an axle but dismissed the thought because he didn't want to distract her. They didn't have time to worry about the suspension on the truck.

Three times they were forced to squeeze onto the shoulder to allow trucks leaving Fort Brida to pass them. Corban was relieved to see every vehicle was packed with Strays, three or four in the cab and fifteen or more in the bed. Each time she let a truck by, Nikki avoided the ditch by centimeters, but as the road became rougher the closer they got to Brida, Corban wasn't sure if their luck would hold.

When the gates of the fort came into view, Corban noticed the time on the dashboard and touched Nikki's shoulder. *I've never made this drive in less than an hour.*

Twenty-eight minutes is too long. Nikki's knuckles were white as she gripped the shuddering steering wheel, pushing the truck to its limits. She hit a rut at full speed, and Corban's head bounced against the ceiling of the cab.

He gripped the door handle with his free hand and tried to breathe. *What's the plan?*

First thing we do is find Mom and Derek and tell them to get the darkness out of Brida. Nikki sped through the open gates and parked in the center of the courtyard. She vaulted from the cab and shouted, "Take it!" to a group of people attempting to squeeze into an already full Tailors Guild truck.

Corban slid from his seat and watched a dozen Strays hurry over, Frieda Moul and Bertram Conquist among them.

"I need to wait for Solona!" Bertram told Corban when he reached the passenger's side door. "She's gathering medical supplies from the infirmary!"

Corban saw the other trucks leaving in a hurry. He didn't know if any more were en route to help with the evacuation. "Go! I'll make sure she's safe!"

Bertram hesitated.

"Go!" Corban pushed him inside the cab. "Do you think I'd let anything happen to Nikki's mother? I promise I'll get her to shelter!"

Corban locked eyes with Nikki on the other side of the hood and realized why he was searching for her in his premonition.

She seemed to reach the same conclusion. "We need to split up to find Mom and Derek, don't we?"

"We should stay together." He knew it was an impossible goal, but he needed to say it. The Cooks Guild truck backed away, opening the space between them. Corban moved toward Nikki, but she shook her head.

"You check the infirmary. I'll check Mom's apartment."

The first rumble of thunder drowned out Corban's protest.

"There's no time to argue!" Nikki was already in motion. "Meet me on the third floor of the north wall," she called over her shoulder.

TWENTY-ONE
REFUGE

"Excuse me." Thane tried not to bump people with the cooler as he cut ahead of the line, working his way up the ramp. "The hospital isn't a storm shelter. Please take refuge in one of the other ships," he told the scowling man at the airlock.

The Stray stopped pounding on the door and turned to Thane, his stance aggressive. "So why are you here?"

Thane didn't know this person he'd already nick-named Grumpy in his mind, but he recognized the fear in the man's tone. "I'm delivering food for the medical staff and patients. I'm not staying. Excuse me." Thane set the cooler on the landing in front of the airlock and nudged Grumpy out of the way so he could reach the keypad beside the round door.

He started to tap in the code but stopped before pressing the last number. He frowned over his shoulder at the people on the gangway, including Grumpy, who refused to budge. Thane raised his voice and announced to everyone in line, "The hospital isn't a storm shelter. The beds are reserved for anyone who's sick or injured. Please take refuge in one of the other ships."

There was some grumbling, but people made their way down the gangway and did as instructed.

He waited until Grumpy exited the ramp before pressing the last button on the keypad. The large round door cycled open. Thane scanned the tarmac with his eyes and ears before stepping inside the entryway, but there was no sign of his brother.

Thane knew Corban intended to go to Fort Brida as soon as he could get away. The difficult part was accepting the fact that nothing Thane did would stop Corban from risking his life, or Nikki's. The premonition would happen exactly the way Corban saw it, and nothing anyone tried to do would change the outcome. It was frustrating, but it was the grim reality of Corban's Talent. Thane figured he should be used to the uncertainty by now, but what unnerved him the most was the sense of helplessness. Not knowing what might happen when the dam broke filled him with a level of anxiety he hadn't experienced since Jing was abducted by her father to be taken aboard the *Unity*.

His gaze lingered on the *Unity*'s mountain of ashes, and he vowed not to imagine what might happen at Fort Brida when the storm broke. *There's nothing I can do.*

Dr. Lorna DeKalb roused Thane from his worried thoughts as she approached him in the entryway. "Could you take that up to the galley on level four?"

"Yes, ma'am." Thane lifted the cooler again and started toward the elevator.

"And we'll need a few more boxes of food, if you can grab some off the next truck, Thane," the surgeon called after him.

"I'd be happy to, ma'am."

By the time Thane dropped off the cooler and returned to the tarmac, the Cooks Guild truck was gone. He scanned the voices in the crowd for Jing's as he hurried over to a Farmers Guild truck parked nearby. Several people were hurrying off with crates of food from the bed, but he claimed the last two stacked near the cab. He carried them toward the hospital.

Jing met him at the foot of the gangway. "The library is stocked for at least fifty people. Let me help you." She snatched the top crate from his arms before he could protest and walked ahead of him up the ramp. "Where's Corban and Nikki?"

He couldn't tell from her tone if she was concerned. When he didn't answer, she frowned at him over her shoulder. "They didn't leave for Brida, did they?"

"I don't hear their voices—since you know they can communicate without words—but, yes, I think they did."

Now she was concerned. Jing stopped at the top of the ramp and turned to him with flushed cheeks. "But the dam's going to break! We have to stop them!"

Thane started to say "we can't" but a huge rumble of thunder drowned out his words. "It's too late," he said when there was a break in the noise.

Jing studied the sky, which changed from pewter gray to inky black in minutes. "We can't let them—!"

"There's nothing we can do, *meili.*" Thane stepped past her into the ship's entryway. "We'll get caught in the storm if we try to leave now."

Jing bit her lip and followed him to the lift without another word of protest. He hoped her calm-in-a-crisis personality would take over soon because he doubted his ability to keep his emotions in check much longer.

Thane recalled the last time they were on this ship together. Jing was unconscious when he'd carried her aboard minutes after the *Unity* exploded. Solona—with a gunshot wound in her thigh—had wrestled Jing away from Kun Kaczenski and dragged Jing to safety across the tarmac on her lab coat. It had been a close call, one that still haunted Thane.

Keep it together, he told himself as the thunder increased in volume and intensity.

He and Jing discovered Yasmin Conquist in the fourth level galley. She was moving fish from the cooler to the refrigerator, using one hand. The other was pinching her nose shut. "You can set them here." Yasmin pointed to an empty stretch of counter in the tiny room. "I hope we have some vegetables to go with all this celadon trout."

"You do." Thane set his crate down and helped Jing with hers. "Is Rupert here too?"

Yasmin nodded. "I convinced Dr. DeKalb he could help out, especially since I'm not feeling well."

"Why aren't you—?" Jing began but stopped short when Yasmin flashed an awkward grin. "Are you—?"

"We found out yesterday," Yasmin said. "Rupert insisted I get tested after I threw up on his shoes!"

It took Thane a moment to figure out what the women were laughing about but managed a "Congratulations!" after Jing gave him a searching look.

"Thank goodness I can tune out my Talent, or I wouldn't be able to stand close to this fish." Yasmin kept a firm grip on her nose, but Thane noticed fresh beads of perspiration on her forehead.

"We can finish putting the food away." Jing stepped over to the refrigerator and gave the nurse a gentle push toward the doorway. "Go lie down or something."

"Thank you!" Yasmin bolted from the galley without further encouragement.

Thane grinned. The news that his best friend was going to be a father eased his tension a fraction. He and Jing set to work, putting away the food from the crates they'd brought aboard. He handed her lettuce, tomatoes, broccoli, carrots, blueberries, goat's milk, oranges, lemons, and a box of eggs to store in the refrigerator while he placed bags of quinoa, oats, sweet potatoes, and cornmeal in an overhead cabinet.

"Pickles go in the fridge?" He held up a canning jar labeled *dill*.

Jing shrugged and took the jar from him. "Solona should be here."

Thane arched an eyebrow at her for the random comment. "Corban and Nikki should be here too, but there's nothing we can do about it."

Jing frowned and closed the fridge. "We should probably take shelter in the library." Another boom of thunder emphasized her words.

He nodded, resigned, and took her hand. They rode the lift to the entryway and found Dr. DeKalb staring out the open airlock. The rain was coming down hard. A sudden gust of wind plastered their clothes to their bodies.

The doctor cycled the door shut on the storm and turned to face them. "You two can shelter here."

"Are you sure?" Thane asked. "We could run to the library."

"I'm sure." DeKalb gave them a wry smile. "I have an appendectomy patient in recovery, a woman in labor— and her husband's making such a fuss I might have to sedate him—a cracked skull in ICU, and somehow three of my five nurses have morning sickness."

"Three!" Jing laughed.

"Yes, it seems the Strays are taking Solona's advice to heart." DeKalb's smile morphed into a frown. "She left in a hurry after the surgery, but I thought she'd get back before the storm broke."

Thane was tempted to tell the surgeon where Solona was, but he didn't want to worry her. "I'm sure she'd be here if she wasn't needed elsewhere."

"That's right," Jing said. "I'm sure Eliana needed her since she's pregnant with twins."

"Twins?" Thane sputtered.

DeKalb nodded. "I heard." She gave Thane a mischievous wink, which he didn't appreciate, but it made Jing giggle. "If you two can manage the galley during the storm, that would be a big help."

"We're happy to help wherever you need us, ma'am," Thane said. "We'll find an empty cabin and plan a menu." He took Jing's elbow and steered her back to the lift.

"I know how to make grilled cheese," Jing whispered. "That's all."

He waited until the doors closed before admitting, "I can't cook either. Corban and I ate all our meals in the dining hall."

"Rupert?" they said in unison.

Thane gave a weak laugh and drew Jing into a tight embrace. The anxiety felt like a heavy weight in his chest. "We won't know anything until the storm's over."

There were no tears in Jing's eyes. Her petite body was solid in his arms, supporting him. "I've never done much praying, but I think now would be a good time to start."

"It'll be all right." Thane was talking more to himself than to Jing. "They'll survive."

"Of course they will." She went up on tiptoe to give him a firm kiss. "Corban saw himself and Nikki with a baby, and his premonitions are never wrong."

The weight in Thane's chest eased. "That's right! I forgot!"

Jing smiled. "It's a good thing you have me around to remind you."

TWENTY-TWO
STORM

Nikki put everything else out of her mind as she raced across the courtyard to Brida's east wall. She pushed open the door to the first-floor hallway and hurried to apartment 8E. "Mom!" She pounded on the door. "Solona!" She tried the doorknob, but it was locked. *Where is she?*

She took off toward the dining hall, figuring it was worth a try. Normally the cooks distributed all the food from the kitchens so people had the provisions they needed for the three-day storm, but Nikki knew this wasn't a normal storm. Evacuating Brida had been top priority.

Now would be a good time to send me a message, Derek! Nikki wished for the umpteenth time that she had a useful Talent like her brother-in-law's. She kept her head on a swivel, searching for stragglers as she ran. She wasn't sure what to do if she found someone, since it appeared their Cooks Guild truck was the last vehicle to evacuate, but she didn't have time to worry about it.

"Mom!" She pushed open the door to the empty dining hall and ran straight back to the kitchen. "Derek?" The power to the fort was off, so the kitchen was dark. Nikki forced herself to stop and listen, but it was obvious the place was deserted.

Another deafening rumble of thunder urged her to keep moving. She turned and ran back outside to the courtyard. "Solona! Derek!" A powerful gust of wind almost swept her off her feet, and the storm broke. The rain came down in sheets, soaking her to the skin.

Nikki abandoned the search, turning her attention to the north wall. She fought the punishing winds and rain to reach the stairs to the upper floors, and shouldered the door open.

She took a moment to catch her breath inside the dry stairwell. Nikki pushed her dripping hair away from her face and wrung out the hem of her shirt. She hoped Corban was having better luck locating Derek. From his premonition, Nikki knew she would find her mother.

Nikki ascended the stone stairs to the dimly lit third-floor hallway. Token emergency lights cast a weak glow over the entrances to the stairwells at either end, but it was pitch dark in the middle of the hall. She headed into the darkness, assuming she'd be able to locate the apartment where Sergey, Linnea, and the other telekinetic Strays gathered to wait for the flood. She strained to hear voices, but the storm was too loud. *Corban said he put out his left hand and fell into the apartment.*

Nikki stopped short. *But was he moving east or west down the hall?* She sighed and opted for a more practical solution by approaching the nearest door and knocking. She pounded hard to be heard over the booming thunder, but there was no answer.

She moved on to the next apartment and used the sides of her fists to bang on the door.

After eight doors, her hands ached. *This isn't working.* Fortunately, the ninth door to apartment 35N flew open at her touch.

"Nikki, you shouldn't be here!" Linnea Savoy admitted her into the dark exterior apartment.

"Neither should you!" Nikki squinted, trying to make out the other faces. The window was shuttered, the only light provided by an oil lamp on a bedside table. She recognized Sergey Gupta from the reception, but the rest were strangers to her.

"We're staying," Sergey put an arm around Linnea's waist. "If the dam breaks, we'll stop the flood."

Nikki bit her lip. "I don't doubt your Talents or your courage, but do you seriously think you can stop hundreds of thousands of liters of water?"

"I don't know, but we have to try," Sergey said.

"We were able to move the river yesterday when Solona had us practice," Linnea said. "It worked for a few minutes."

"You stopped the river?" Nikki was unable to keep the skepticism from her tone.

Linnea dropped her eyes. "Not exactly, no, but we did slow it down a little."

Nikki bit back a sarcastic response. "Speaking of Solona, have any of you seen her?"

Sergey grimaced. "She's on the roof, keeping an eye on the dam."

"Isaac's with her," Linnea added before Nikki asked.

"But it's pouring!" Nikki said. "Not even a vision Talent could see through this monsoon!"

A dark-skinned young man standing near the boarded-up window chimed in. "We told her, but she insisted on keeping watch with Isaac."

"They're probably half-drowned by now." Nikki turned back toward the hallway. "I'm going to talk some sense into her."

"But—" Linnea called after her, but Nikki didn't look back as she dashed down the hall to a door labeled *roof access*.

The door opened to a closet-sized space that housed a simple wooden ladder mounted to the opposite wall. Nikki climbed to the ceiling and raised the hatch to the roof. Chilly water poured through the opening, drenching her as she scrambled out onto the rampart. She pushed the hatch back into place before the ladder well flooded but thought the effort was a lost cause since the roof was already ankle-deep in water.

"Mom!" A powerful gust of wind propelled Nikki toward the battlements. She staggered, fighting the gale to reach Solona and Isaac, who were wearing rain gear but clinging to a pair of crenels to keep from being blown off the roof.

"Mom!" Nikki threw both arms around the crenel to Solona's right. "Get back inside before you drown!"

Solona shook her head, but her words were lost in a deafening rumble of thunder.

Isaac, who was crouched to the left of Solona, looked over at Nikki with a resigned expression. Nikki assumed he'd be easier to convince to get out of the rain. As far as she knew, no colonist had ever stayed outside during a storm, and it was suicidal to attempt it.

She hesitated before reaching over to grasp Solona's arm. Her mother's memories filled her mind, forcing Nikki to wrestle her both physically and mentally. "Help me!" she shouted to Isaac.

He moved over to grasp Solona's other arm, and together they dragged her backward, toward the hatch. Nikki was relieved her mother didn't resist. Isaac released Solona's arm, crawled the last meter to the hatch, and lifted it open. He offered Solona a hand, and she took it. She lowered her legs through the hole, found a foothold on the ladder, and descended.

Isaac extended a helping hand to Nikki, but she shook her head and lowered herself to the ladder without assistance. Isaac followed, pulling the hatch shut as soon as he was clear. In moments, they were standing in the third-floor hallway, creating three large puddles on the floor.

"Keeping a lookout won't work, Mom. No one can be outside in this." Nikki thought Solona and Isaac appeared as drenched as she was despite their rain gear. "We'll have to listen for the dam to break."

"In that case, where's Thane?" Solona asked. "We need his help."

Nikki reined in her temper with effort. "He's at the landing strip with Jing. Anywhere is safer than here."

"None of us should be here," Isaac said.

"At last! Someone with common sense!" Nikki gave him a soggy thumbs-up.

"Well, it's too late to leave now, even if we had transportation." Solona swept off her rain hat, showering more droplets across the slippery floor.

Nikki shivered. "Mom, you don't really think the Strays can stop the fort from being flooded?"

"I honestly don't know." Solona's defensiveness was growing. "But they insisted on trying. Staying wasn't my idea, and it took time to convince Robin Aziz to go to Waterfall with her husband and baby. None of the others would listen to me."

Nikki wasn't satisfied with her explanation. "Where's Derek?"

"He left an hour ago for your apartment." Solona drew herself up to her full height, which didn't quite reach Nikki's shoulder. "Do you think I'd let him stay here and make Eliana a widow?"

"But it's all right if *you* stay and make me an orphan?" Nikki snapped.

"Ladies, let's find some towels before we catch pneumonia. We can debate which of you is crazier with the other doomed volunteers." Isaac started down the hall to 35N.

Nikki was taken aback by Isaac's sarcasm but didn't blame him for being terrified. "Did Mom give you the option of evacuating?"

Solona threw her a scowl. "I didn't tell him to stay."

Nikki snorted. "You have this way of *persuading* people to do things. Thane told us you assigned him, Isaac, and Zhao to inspect the dam."

"And it's a good thing I did, otherwise the entire population of this fort would be in harm's way!" Solona said.

"*If* we're in harm's way." Isaac pushed open the door to the apartment and held it for Nikki and Solona. "The dam might not break until the next storm."

"It'll break during this storm," Nikki told the room. "Corban heard it in his premonition."

"Speaking of Corban—" Solona's eyes swept the room. "Has anyone seen him?"

Linnea handed out towels to Nikki, Solona, and Isaac. "He hasn't been here."

"He went to check the infirmary," Nikki said. "That's where Bertram told us you were."

Solona shed her raincoat and wrapped a towel around her shoulders. "I had to tell Bert something, or he would've insisted on staying."

Nikki was shivering too hard to chastise her mom for lying to her boyfriend. She rubbed the towel over her dripping hair, but her feet were going numb. "You wouldn't happen to have a blanket?" she asked Linnea.

"How about some dry clothes?" The Stray pushed

a bundle of fabric into her hands. "There's a candle burning in the bathroom."

Nikki needed no urging. She dried as much as she could in the bathroom and put on a set of clothes, which were probably Linnea's because the jeans hit well above her ankles. Nikki resisted putting her sodden shoes back on and walked into the main room in dry socks.

An extra loud rumble of thunder was followed by a long crackling sound and a shuddering crash, which reverberated through the fortress walls. Nikki had never heard trees come down so early into a storm and tried not to let the fear show on her face as she studied the room.

Her eyes adjusted to the dim lighting, and she took a head count. Besides herself, Solona, Isaac, Linnea, and Sergey, there were ten people she didn't recognize huddled against the walls or sitting on the bed, wide-eyed and tight-lipped. The tension in the room was thick enough to cut with a knife.

"Where's Corban?" Nikki asked right as another tree came down with a mighty crash outside the apartment. "Darkness! He's out in this!"

"I'll help you find him." Solona slipped her raincoat back on.

"Take mine." Isaac handed Nikki his poncho. It was dripping, but she accepted it, knowing it would offer some insulation against the deluge.

"Thanks." Nikki was reluctant to slide her feet back into her soaked shoes and follow Solona out into the hall. As soon as she shut the door behind them, she told her mom, "In his premonition, Corban shows up here and asks where I am."

"Then maybe we shouldn't wander far." Solona

started toward the east stairwell.

Nikki noticed a distinct change in her mother's tone from defensive to fearful. She fell into step beside her. "Do you have a plan for stopping this flood?"

"No." Solona's shoulders slumped. "I wasn't firm enough. I should've told everyone to evacuate. I should've insisted it's too dangerous. This is my fault for organizing the stupid merging Talents experiments. Now Strays think they have super powers."

"We don't think that! Didn't you see their expressions, Linnea and the others? They're terrified. They wish they were anywhere but here."

"But it's too late to take shelter somewhere else." Solona sounded bitter. "I've read about floods on Earth. Water can move everything in its path. Trees, buildings, cities, entire islands have been washed away by floods. That slime worm Leighton Abrams threw this fort together in a few months. Brida doesn't stand a chance against the Cold River."

Nikki racked her brain, trying to remember something she'd read about changing the course of a river. *Or was it a sea?* "Darkness!" She froze, ignoring the door to the stairwell Solona was holding open for her. "No, the flood can't be stopped, but it could be diverted!"

"What are you talking about?"

"It's been done before! A sea—the Red Sea! It was parted! The water was separated on each side so it went around—"

"You're talking about *Moses?*" Solona interrupted with a derisive snort. "That's not telekinetics; it was an act of God—a miracle! We don't have any miracles on Vesta!"

Nikki set her jaw. "Well, maybe it's time we asked for one!"

TWENTY-THREE
FLOOD

There was no sign of anyone in the infirmary or the apothecary. Both places were unlocked but empty. No one bothered to barricade the doors or windows in their haste to evacuate Brida.

Corban gave up the search and made his way to the south wall stairwell. The darkness was illuminated by a jagged fork of lightning, allowing him a split second to see his destination. He winced as a deafening boom of thunder came right after the lightning, but he wasn't concerned for his own safety as he took a deep breath, plunged into the storm, and sprinted across the open courtyard. He ran blindly through the driving rain, dodging obstacles such as fire pits and picnic tables. The wind pushed back at him, plastering his clothes to his body, and the torrential rain felt like needles against his skin.

Another flash of lightning offered him a glimpse of his goal: the stairs to the upper floors of the north wall. Corban fought the storm a few more meters before wrenching open the door and stumbling into the dark stairwell. He didn't pause to appreciate being out of the punishing elements as he took the stone steps three at a time. Soaked to the skin, he shivered from both cold and fear as he burst through the door into the dimly lit, third-floor hallway.

"Nikki!" He heard the fear in his own voice. "Nikki!"

He strained his ears, desperate to hear a reply, but the thunder, howling winds, and hammering rain on the roof drowned out all other noises. He reached to his left until he located the wall and used it as a guide to make his way down the hall. "*Nikki!*"

A door beneath his hand swung open, and Corban fell sideways into an apartment. A pair of hands seized him under the arms and hoisted him to his feet.

"What are you doing here?" Sergey asked. "You don't even live in Brida. Why didn't you evacuate with the rest of the fort?"

"I couldn't leave without Nikki!" Corban turned to face Sergey. "Have you seen her?"

"She left a few minutes ago to look for you. Solona went with her." Linnea's gentle voice was tinged with fear. "We'd help you look, but we have to be ready."

Corban was aware of several more people in the apartment, their nervous voices muted by the storm raging outside, making it impossible for him to identify them. "Who else is here, and why did you stay behind?"

"I'm here to keep watch."

He noticed Isaac Nomura for the first time. His former roommate was sitting on the floor, a towel wrapped around his shoulders. Water dripped from the ends of Isaac's black hair as if he'd just come in from the storm too. "Obviously it's impossible to see anything once the rain started."

They all heard a noise that drowned out the storm and the splintering thud of trees coming down. There was a roaring boom in the distance, outside the fort, similar to the *Unity*'s explosion.

"Get to the roof!" Sergey shouted.

Panic shot through Corban. "*Nikki!* I have to find her!"

"*Corban!*" Nikki burst into the apartment with Solona on her heels.

"Out of the way!" Sergey shouted. He and the other Strays were in motion, heading for the door. "The water will reach us in minutes!"

"Wait!" Nikki held out her arms, blocking the doorway. "You can't do this from the roof! Stay here! Open the shutters!"

"Nikki, what are you—?" Corban stammered.

"I've got an idea! Just trust me!" Her voice was shrill. "Hurry! I need six of you here and six in the apartment next door! Corban, go with them!"

"What do I—?" he started to ask, but Nikki grabbed his arm and rushed him into the hallway, along with Sergey, Linnea, Isaac, and four other Strays.

Her plan filled his mind like an uploaded datafile in the few moments they had contact. *Understand?* Nikki thought. *They have to send the water to the left. The left!*

Corban didn't have a chance to acknowledge her mental instructions before he was in the hallway. "Next door!" he shouted to Sergey.

The older Stray turned right and seized the doorknob to 33N. "It's locked!"

"Kick it down!" Corban yelled.

"It's all right, we've got it," Linnea said. She and Sergey stared at the door, and it tore free from its hinges, falling inward with a crash.

"Right." Corban felt stupid. *Of course they can move a door.* The group rushed inside the dark apartment. "Uncover the window! Hurry!"

The telekinetics crossed the room. The shutters shot from the window frame as if pulled by invisible chains and scattered across the floor. The storm blasted its way through the square windowless opening, drenching the room and its occupants.

Isaac looked past Corban to get a glimpse outside. "The flood's almost here!"

"There's no time to explain!" Corban shouted. "Line up as close as you can to the window!"

Sergey and the others scrambled to comply, even as the wind and rain lashed them, making it difficult to get close to the opening.

Corban shouted. "Concentrate on moving the water *to the left*! Don't try to stop it, just focus on moving it to the left!"

"Hold hands!" Linnea shrieked. "Tell Nikki they have to hold hands!"

"I'll do it." Isaac left in a hurry.

The others appeared confused, but there was no time to ask questions. They lined up near the window opening, clasped hands, and focused on the wall of water coming toward Fort Brida.

Corban drew back a few steps. He felt like a coward, knowing there was no escape. If the telekinetics failed to move the flood, they would all drown. The water would wash the fort away as easily as it was leveling the forest between Waterfall and Brida.

The thunderous snapping of trees and the roar of water filled Corban's ears, growing louder until he couldn't hear anything else. He shut his eyes, wishing Nikki was by his side. If they were all going to die, he wanted his last moments to be with her.

TWENTY-FOUR
TSUNAMI

"To the right!" Nikki shrieked. "Concentrate on moving the water to the right!" She heard Solona draw a shuddering breath behind her, but Nikki didn't have time to feel afraid.

"Hold hands!" Isaac bellowed, charging into the room. He slipped on the wet floor and fell to his knees.

Nikki didn't need to ask because it seemed so logical. "Yes, hold hands!"

Six Strays, all strangers to her, stood in a line in front of the window frame and gripped each other's hands, even as the storm fought to push them backward. No one murmured a word against Nikki's crazy idea. She was in awe of their courage. This was a suicidal attempt, and everyone knew it.

Despite the darkness and driving rain, when the river tsunami drew close, it was impossible not to see. It was high enough to reach their window ledge. Entire trees churned in the raging water. Nikki knew it would fill the apartment, drowning them all. She screamed to be heard above the roar of the water. "Concentrate!"

Time seemed to stand still as the raging wall of

death came within meters of Brida's outer wall before it began to shift. It was drawing closer, but it was flowing to the right as if it had met a giant invisible barrier.

"That's it!" Nikki shrieked. "You can do it!" She was terrified the wave would break over them, that it had come too close to Brida to be diverted from its deadly path, but she shut her eyes and offered a silent prayer of desperation. *Please, God! Help them move the water!*

The roaring filled her ears, but Nikki's mind was blanketed by an inexplicable calm. *The wave's not going to flood this room. It's not going to wash away the fort.* She remembered something—an earlier premonition.

Corban and I will have a baby together! We're not going to drown!

Solona gasped. "It's working!"

Nikki's eyes flew open wide. The water she saw through the window was flowing to their right. The churning black wave shifted its path, its strength divided. She moved closer to the line of telekinetics and peered over some shoulders. Despite the torrential rain, she saw the water level dropping below the second-floor windows.

The remainder of the wave broke against the outer wall, causing the floor to shudder, but the fortress held. The water level continued to drop as if a giant had pulled the plug on Vesta's largest bathtub.

"It worked!" She shut her eyes again, offered a silent *thank you,* and raced to the apartment next door. Corban met her in the hallway, and they almost knocked each other down as they came together in a crushing embrace.

Corban was shaking. *The water shifted to the left! Isaac said the flood parted, just like—!*

Just like Moses parted the Red Sea! Nikki finished. *It's a miracle!*

***

"We'll have plenty of time to survey the damage once the storm's over." Solona wasted no time ushering the exhausted Strays to drier apartments. "It's survival mode for the next three days. The inside corner apartments are the safest." She divided the group into fours and sent them on their way. "If there's no food, break into the apartments on either side. We'll apologize to the owners later."

"Wait," Nikki called after Sergey and Linnea. "Someone needs to unlock this door first!"

The couple walked back to them with weary grins. They were soaking wet and shivering, and Linnea appeared to be in pain as she pressed a hand to her forehead.

Sergey touched the doorknob of 31N, and the lock clicked open. "There you go."

"Thank you." Nikki wanted to say more but words failed her as the couple turned away, heading toward 31E.

"Light." Isaac led the way into the hexagon-shaped apartment and lit the oil lamp on a little two-person table by the kitchenette.

"Fridge!" Corban went to survey the contents, but Nikki was more interested in locating towels. The single outside wall was barely wide enough to include a window, but she was grateful to see that whoever lived here took the time to secure the shutters.

There were two towels in the bathroom, but there were several blankets in the wardrobe. Nikki shed all her wet clothes in the bathroom, wrapped a blanket around herself from head to toe, and was asleep as soon as she lay down on one of the twin beds, oblivious to the storm that raged outside.

TWENTY-FIVE
LIFE AND LOSS

Thane pulled the pan out of the oven and studied the steaming trout filets. "Do these look done to you, *meili*?"

Jing paused at the cutting board where she was dicing tomatoes. "Looks done, but I've never baked fish before. Ask Rupert."

"He told me eight or nine minutes was long enough." Thane set the pan on the stovetop.

"I'm sure it's fine. Let's fill some bowls. Dr. DeKalb said Mallik is ready for solid food," Jing said, referring to the appendectomy patient from East Fort. She scooped the tomatoes off the cutting board and spread them over a bowl of chopped lettuce. "We can put a piece of fish on top of each salad and use some of the citrus dressing Rupert made earlier."

"The storm should be over in a few hours." Thane didn't mean to speak the thought aloud. He glimpsed her face in his peripheral vision, gauging her reaction.

"I hope so." Jing blinked a few times, but her voice remained steady.

Over the past three days, they'd made an effort not

to speculate about Nikki, Corban, Solona, and the others at Fort Brida. Light conversation, even if forced, became their mutual goal. Thane found silence a more practical goal for himself, but he knew how difficult it was for Jing to keep her feelings bottled up.

He also knew worrying wouldn't make the storm end any sooner, but it was getting harder to stifle his anxiety. He didn't tell Jing he'd heard the dam collapse soon after the storm broke. Although his hearing range was limited to two kilometers, the sound of a fifty meter high concrete wall giving way was loud enough to detect over the howling storm. Another one of Corban's premonitions had become a reality, but being forced to wait three days to learn the outcome was almost unbearable.

"I doubt we'll be able to reach Brida unless we hike," Jing said. "Any trucks that survived out on the tarmac will need recharging, and the roads will be solid mud and debris, basically impassible." Her light tone didn't match her furrowed brow.

"I'm sure we can borrow a bike."

"A canoe might work better." Jing sniffled for the first time in days. "I wish Rupert or Derek was there, someone to send us a message."

Thane was determined to offer her, and himself, some hope. "If we get close enough, I might be able to hear their voices."

Jing put down the carrot she was peeling and turned to face him, her eyes filled with unshed tears. "How close?"

"Waterfall—maybe."

"It's more than two kilometers from Brida."

"It's worth a try." Thane doubted they'd be able to travel any farther south than Waterfall. It was likely everything below the dam had flooded. He held out his arms to Jing, and she stepped into the embrace without hesitation.

"As soon as the rain stops," she murmured, "we're heading to Waterfall."

***

The rain continued to lash the hospital on day four. Thane had experienced two four-day storms in his lifetime and wasn't surprised this early storm was taking longer, but the extra time added to his anxiety. His stress level had ratcheted up from unbearable to borderline panic. Jing gave up any pretense at light conversation and was shedding tears by lunchtime. Thane spent a lot of time consoling her and found that focusing on her comfort helped ease his own fears a little.

Rupert took one look at Jing when he stopped by the galley at dinnertime and said, "Let me take over here."

"But—" Thane set down the spoon he was using to stir the quinoa, which looked too dry to be edible.

Rupert ushered both of them to the door. "I'll bring Yasmin some ginger tea later. You two take a break."

Thane gave his friend a helpless shrug and followed Jing from the galley. He climbed the central ladder after her to level six and their cabin, which was one of the rare post-op rooms with two beds and a port window.

Jing took one look at the storm outside and erupted in fresh sobs. Thane went to her and wrapped her in a comforting embrace. He patted her back and made shushing noises until she quieted to sniffles and hiccups.

"They're fine," he whispered. "Remember the baby premonition?"

She nodded. "I need to see for myself they're all right."

"We will," Thane knew he was assuring himself as much as he was reassuring Jing.

They stood there for a long time, staring out at the rain.

Thane made an effort to sound optimistic. "Looks like it's slowing down a little."

"I need to tell you something."

It was a random comment, but Thane humored her. "What?"

"I'm late."

Thane needed a moment to process this. He wanted to say, "Late for what?" but suspected it was the wrong response. He was reminded of how little he knew about women and said nothing, hoping she'd offer him a clue.

Jing harrumphed. "My cycle is late."

All the air left his lungs. "You're—?"

"I don't know." There was an impatient edge to her tone. "But since we're on the hospital ship, I could get tested." Jing squirmed free of his embrace and tilted her head back to look into his face. "Shall we go see Dr. DeKalb?"

Thane knew he should say something enthusiastic, but he was in shock. As he stalled, trying to wrap his mind around this stunning possibility, Jing's half-smile turned into a half-frown.

He had an idea. Thane gripped Jing's shoulders and steered her backward toward one of the beds. "We don't need to see Dr. DeKalb yet. Lie down."

The frown turned into a scowl as she sat on the edge of the hospital bed. "What are you doing? I'm not in the mood—"

Thane almost laughed. "Not that, *meili*. Just lie down." He lifted her legs, swung them up onto the mattress, and pushed her gently onto her back. "I want to listen."

Jing's mouth formed a cute *O* of surprise. "You think you can hear—"

"I can try." Thane got down on his good knee beside the bed, turned his head to the side so he could see her face, and pressed one ear to her abdomen.

"Lower, below my navel," Jing whispered.

She shook with giggles for a moment, but he did as she suggested, repositioning his ear. Thane closed his eyes and focused his Talent. He heard the gurgling of her stomach and intestines; a whoosh-whoosh as her heart valves opened and closed, moving blood through her veins; and a sound like tiny bellows as air inflated and deflated her lungs. All the sounds were muffled, as if underwater, but he tuned them out and concentrated, searching for something different.

It didn't take long to find it. It was soft, like the fluttering of an insect's wings heard from a great distance.

Thane let out a breath he didn't realize he was holding. He raised himself onto his elbows, looked Jing in the eye, and nodded, unable to speak.

"I hope it's a boy," she whispered.

He took both her hands in his. "I don't care what it is, only that it's ours."

Jing started to laugh. "You look a bit pale, Dad. You should lie down before you keel over."

***

It stopped raining during the night, but Thane didn't notice until Jing nudged him awake and said, "We should cook breakfast."

He stared out their port window at the gray sky, which was beginning to lighten to a watery blue. "And then we'll head to Waterfall."

"I hope you brought your hip waders." Jing smiled at him, the first real smile he'd seen from her the entire storm. "There's probably a pair stashed here in one of the lockers."

"You said the hospital was a treasure trove for abandoned things. That's how you and Nikki were able to disguise me as an old man to sneak inside Waterfall."

"Yes, back when you and Corban were fugitives, hiding from your uncle."

Thane sobered at the mention of his uncle Leighton. "He deliberately built Fort Brida below the dam, knowing it would flood if the dam ever collapsed. He was an evil slime worm. It's hard to believe he and my dad were brothers."

Jing pulled on her shoes. "You're not the only one who had a slime worm for a father."

"Let's not go there." Thane grimaced. "Let's talk about a new generation of Abrams, beginning with our baby."

Jing opened the door to their cabin. "We should name *him* after your father." She flashed a teasing grin.

"Maybe we should name *her* after your mother."

Jing's smile vanished. "It has to be a boy."

"It doesn't matter, *meili*." Thane captured her hand as they headed out into the corridor. "Don't fret about being a grandmother when you're not even a mother yet."

She threw him a sour look but didn't say anything else as they descended the ladder to the galley.

They found Rupert at the stove, hard at work on a skillet of scrambled eggs. A second skillet of cornbread was cooling on the counter at his elbow.

"You aren't supposed to do the cooking." Thane attempted to take the spatula from him, but Rupert sidestepped the move.

"I've got breakfast under control. You two are probably anxious to get to Brida." Rupert turned off the burner and faced them with a stern expression. "I sent messages to Corban, Nikki, and Solona, telling them to expect you by nightfall."

Jing gawked. "How presumptuous of you."

"Yes, it'll take us at least half an hour to search the lockers for hip waders and an inflatable boat," Thane said.

"Yasmin said this place might have both." Rupert filled two plates with eggs and wedges of cornbread, and pushed them into Thane's and Jing's hands. "Good luck."

***

An hour later, Thane and Jing were ready to leave the hospital. They were both wearing an odd assortment of clothing since neither had brought anything with them to the ship. Jing wore an oversized trench coat over pink nurse's scrubs and a pair of waterproof bluedeer-skin boots that reached her knees. Thane had a difficult time finding anything that fit well, so he settled for black scrubs, a hooded purple jacket too small to zip, and his own hunting boots, with an extra pair of socks to keep his feet dry for a few kilometers. He found a child's backpack and filled it with four water bottles, a few oranges, a large hunting knife, a waterproof tarp, and a folding shovel.

Their most valuable find was a sturdy-looking bike

in a storage room off the entryway, hidden behind the extra gurneys and wheelchairs. By the time they were able to move everything to reach the bike, they were both anxious to leave.

Thane slipped one arm through a strap of the backpack, since it was too small to extend to both shoulders, and opened the airlock door.

The landing strip was littered with tree limbs and debris. A few brave colonists had emerged from the ships and were examining the half dozen trucks that hadn't blown onto their sides during the storm. Thane didn't want to waste time joining them, checking to see if any of the engines would start, because he knew the vehicles' batteries were dead. He pushed the bike down the gangway and stood on the damp tarmac.

Jing climbed onto the seat. "I'll pedal."

Thane was tempted to argue, but they both knew his missing kneecap couldn't handle the strain of pedaling a bike. He settled himself between the handlebars, grateful the route to Brida was mostly downhill.

"Once we reach the road, or what's left of it, it'll be solid mud, *meili*. Take a break whenever you need to. We'll walk if it gets too thick."

Jing didn't answer as she started pedaling. She was out of breath by the time they reached the wide bridge, but she didn't utter a word of complaint.

The Cold River was a few centimeters lower than the bridge, the choppy water filled with storm debris. Thane grimaced at the bloated body of a purple crawler as it passed out of sight beneath the bridge.

The main road connecting the forts was now two parallel gullies so thick with mud that Thane thought walking might be easier. Jing, however, didn't hesitate to steer the bike right into the mud. They got stuck twice, and Thane dug the tires free with the folding shovel. They carried the bike over fallen trees and standing water but kept going. They rode a little, but mostly they walked and pushed the bike.

By midday, they reached the turnoff to West Fort. Thane's left leg was beginning to ache, but he didn't complain. He and Jing were both covered in mud. The slime was working its way inside his boots.

"Maybe we should get something to eat at West," he said.

Jing shook her head. "It'll add two kilometers to our hike."

"You're not hungry?" Thane wondered if it was safe for her to miss a meal. *And at what point does the morning sickness start?* He resolved to learn more about pregnancy so he could be a more supportive husband.

"I'm fine," Jing said. "I won't say no to one of those oranges if you want to peel it for me."

Thane held up his filthy hands with a rueful grin.

Jing showed him her own muddy palms. "Never mind. I can wait."

Thane hoped his leg could endure the additional five kilometers to the next fort. "We can ask the communications sentry to send a message when we reach Waterfall."

"I think we can make it to Brida today," Jing said.

That's wishful thinking. Thane kept his mouth shut.

***

It was late afternoon by the time Waterfall's walls came into view, and they were both hungry, exhausted, and chilled from the mud covering them from head to toe. Thane's leg hurt so much that he knew he'd have to be off his feet for a few days. As they drew closer, they discovered one more problem—there was no way to reach the fort.

"Now what?" Jing groaned.

The dam was completely gone and, with it, the bridge connecting the road to the main gates. They stared at the massive pile of broken concrete, rebar, and shattered trees at the bottom of the falls. The swollen river cascaded over what remained of the natural cliff and flowed over the debris. The Cold River had expanded its shoreline on both sides, creating a new lake past the remains of the dam.

"Awful," Jing muttered. "And everyone in Waterfall is stranded until a bridge can be rebuilt."

"They're not cut off." Thane waved to a lone sentry on the catwalk over the closed gates. "They can reach Greenfield and East Fort from that side of the river." He turned to look over the flattened forest on the far side of the new lake. "They'll have to go on foot though."

"There's no way we can reach Brida on foot." Jing pointed downhill to the spot where the road disappeared, washed away by the flood.

"Not tonight, at least."

"Where are we supposed to stay? We can't be outside a fort at night." Jing bit her lip. "We'll have to go back to West."

"I can't." Thane seated himself on a fallen tree and stretched out his left leg. He didn't like admitting he'd reached his limit, but he took one look at Jing's pale, pinched, mud-smeared face and realized she was spent too. "You need to eat."

Jing nodded, propped the bike next to him, and sighed. "What'll we do now?"

Thane tried to compose a reassuring answer, but before he opened his mouth, he heard a familiar voice.

"Thane!"

"I hear Corban!" He got to his feet, with care. His leg was throbbing.

"Where?" Jing climbed onto the fallen tree and turned a full circle, searching with her eyes.

"Thane! Over here!"

"I see him!" Jing pointed to the fort.

Thane couldn't believe his eyes. His brother was on the sentries' catwalk, waving like mad. "How did he get there?"

Nikki appeared on the rampart and made her way across the catwalk to Corban's side. "Jing!"

"They're all right." Jing's eyes filled with tears. "They're all right!"

Thane helped her down from the log. He limped after Jing to the edge of the waterfall, where the bridge used to be. "How do we get over there?" he shouted.

Corban and Nikki were both smiling. "It's easy," Nikki called, "with the right help!"

Thane and Jing watched in amazement as Robin Aziz appeared on the rampart. Moments later, Linnea Savoy and Sergey Gupta joined her.

"Jing first!" Robin called. "You need to relax!"

"What in darkness?" Jing shot Thane a nervous look. "What are they going to do?"

Robin, Linnea, and Sergey grasped each other's hands and stared at Jing.

"I think I know." Thane took a step back. "Relax, *meili*, and trust them."

Jing didn't have time to protest before she was rising into the air. "Thane!" she shrieked.

"Relax!" Thane grinned as he watched her float across the river and touch down on the other side, in front of the gates.

Jing sat down hard on the ground, her mouth hanging open in shock.

"Ready, Thane?" Sergey called.

He nodded and tried to relax but found it wasn't easy as he felt a tug at his shoulders, back, and hips as if he was connected to marionette strings. The tugging increased, and he watched his feet leave the ground. His stomach did a flip as he floated across the deep gorge, the waterfall churning below, but his trip was over in moments as he was set down gently on the ground next to Jing. Thane's left leg gave a painful spasm, unable to support his weight, and he fell onto his backside next to her.

Jing flung her arms around him. "Let's never do that again!" There was a touch of hysteria in her voice.

"Yes, ma'am." Thane started to laugh, and she joined in after a moment, her eyes wet with happy tears.

They were both laughing hard when the gates behind them moved inward with a loud creaking of water-logged hinges, the opening chords to a happy family reunion.

TWENTY-SIX
VESTA'S FUTURE

Jing got to her feet and rushed over to Nikki with a happy squeal, but Corban sensed that Thane was hurting. "Sergey, help me?" Corban asked.

"Sure." Sergey and Linnea had come down from the ramparts to greet Thane and Jing, and it took the telekinetics' combined Talents to move the large gates.

Corban and Sergey crouched on either side of Thane and helped him to his feet.

"Can you stand?" Corban kept a grip on his brother's arm, waiting to see if he'd remain upright.

"I'm not sure." Thane pulled free of Sergey's grip and turned to give Corban a rib-cracking hug. "I think I overdid it, but who cares? We're so relieved to see you!"

Nikki and Jing's hug was brief, but then Jing almost toppled both brothers as she gave Corban an enthusiastic squeeze. "I can't believe it! You did it! You stopped the flood!"

"Whoa!" Corban pried himself from his sister-in-law's embrace and secured an arm around Thane's back to keep him from falling. "Nikki and I didn't do

235

anything."

Nikki blinked hard and wiped her eyes on the sleeve of the shirt she'd borrowed from Solona. "Sergey, Linnea, and the other telekinetic Strays stopped it. They were able to part the water so the flood went around Brida."

"But you told us how," Linnea said. "We were scared out of our minds and didn't know what to do."

"Not true," Corban said. "You remembered to have everyone hold hands."

"Physical contact intensifies our combined Talents." Linnea smiled at Nikki. "You and Corban taught us that."

Thane shifted his weight onto his right leg and leaned heavily on Corban's shoulder. "Maybe you should start from the beginning."

"Maybe we should eat first!" Jing said. "I'm exhausted and starving—and I'm eating for two!"

Corban and Nikki's jaws dropped in unison. Nikki sputtered for a moment before rushing to hug Jing again. This time the hug lasted longer. Corban figured Nikki was getting a full report from her best friend/sister-in-law.

"I think food is a good idea," Linnea said. "They've started some cooking fires outside the dining hall, so I'm sure you can get a meal there. Maybe Sergey and I should find out if there are any free rooms for tonight and let you four catch up."

"But—" Sergey started to protest, but Linnea grabbed his arm and marched him inside the fort.

Corban laughed at the flabbergasted expression on Sergey's face. "They're getting married, you know," he told Thane and Jing. "As soon as they can find Mayor Papadopoulos."

"Poor guy won't know what hit him." Thane dodged

a playful swat from Jing.

Jing moved to Thane's other side, although Corban didn't need help as Thane's crutch. Still, Corban understood the need for closeness after all they'd been through the past few days.

Nikki took Corban's free hand, and the four Abrams made their way onto Waterfall's Main Street, moving at Thane's pace. *I'm glad you suggested we come here today, even if it was the hardest hike of my life.* Nikki squeezed his hand.

It was worth it, Corban thought.

"How's Solona?" Thane asked.

"She's fine," Nikki said. "She wasn't happy about part of the cleanup crew sneaking away this morning, but I knew you'd be anxious to see us since there was no way to send you a message. I'm glad we asked Linnea and Sergey to come with us, or we wouldn't have been able to get inside Waterfall."

"I don't care how powerful their Talents are, my feet are staying firmly on the ground from now on!" Jing said.

The other three laughed. "I thought it was fun," Nikki said.

"How's the fort?" Thane asked. "Still standing?"

"Yes, and we're lucky to be alive." Corban fended off the rush of nerves as he recalled the sight of the river tsunami and how close it came to Brida's outer wall.

"I credit divine intervention." Nikki gave his hand a comforting squeeze. "It was a miracle the fort wasn't washed away."

"And us with it." Corban made an effort to slow his pounding heart. They were together again, safe and—*darkness!* "Jing, are you really pregnant?"

"Yes, you're going to be an uncle." Thane laughed.

"You're going to be a father!" Corban said. "I hope you're ready!"

"Don't even joke about how unprepared I am." Thane paused, forcing all of them to stop. "Look around."

They silently took in the storm damage to Waterfall, and at the colonists hard at work sawing fallen trees into manageable logs, repairing downed fences and broken shutters, airing out apartments, picking up debris from the cobblestone streets, and talking to each other while they worked. Some frowned as they focused on tasks, but many were laughing, giving out hugs and hand-shakes, and letting their friends and neighbors know they were grateful to have survived another storm.

"It'll take time to rebuild," Corban said. "But I think the Survivors will take us seriously from now on."

"How will Waterfall generate electricity without the dam?" Jing asked.

Thane shook his head. "I guess the other forts will have to sacrifice some of their solar panels. It'll be in-convenient, but each fort will have the basics for lights and cooking."

"The vehicles won't be able to recharge anymore," Nikki said. "No transportation."

"Linnea said she and Sergey were able to move a truck with their combined Talents," Thane said.

"Darkness," Corban said. "That should surprise me but it doesn't, not after seeing them move the flood."

"Even with all the telekinetics providing transporta-tion, we'll have fewer vehicles on the roads," Jing said.

"Which means we'll be limited to transporting the essentials, like food." Corban nodded.

"Now there's no denying Vesta needs the Strays to survive, and not just because we're adding to the popu-lation." Thane turned his head to kiss Jing on the cheek. "And we're naming her after your mother, *meili*."

Jing's tone was sharp, but she was smiling. "No, we're naming him after your father. Harrison Abrams is a good name."

"All right, we'll call her Harrisona."

"What? We're not naming her that!"

"So you admit it's a girl?" Thane said.

"I didn't say that!"

Corban interrupted their debate with a cheerful announcement. "Food!"

They began moving again toward the dining hall and the half-dozen people who were handing out bowls of steaming stew from a giant pot suspended over a cooking fire.

"As long as their cooking's better than ours," Thane said. "Oh, and we definitely need to wash our hands first."

Jing held up a filthy, mud-coated hand to show the others, and they all started laughing again.

ACKNOWLEDGMENTS

I hope you've enjoyed the Vesta Colony series. Obviously, I could write several more books, but I have other stories demanding my attention right now. Maybe in the future, if there's interest from my readers, I can continue the story of Corban, Nikki, Thane, and Jing, and their children.

If you enjoyed any or all of the three Vesta novels, please consider leaving reviews on Amazon or Goodreads. Since I'm an indie author, reviews make the difference between selling books and toiling in obscurity. I appreciate your support.

I want to thank my family for putting up with my long absences while I barricaded myself in my office to write. Thanks to my beta readers, authors Tamara Ward and Lisa Rector. Lisa also doubles as my editor and formatter, so I couldn't publish without her help. And thanks to my cover artist, Jessica Phillips, who finished the cover six months before I had *Vesta's Survival* written. And a final thank you to my cover models, Jared Weaver and Aaron Weaver.

SterlingRWalker.com